The Mistletoe Haunting

Legend of Minster Lovell

The Mistletoe Haunting

Legend of Minster Lovell

David Slattery-Christy

COSMIC
EGG
BOOKS

Winchester, UK
Washington, USA

First published by Cosmic Egg Books, 2016
Cosmic Egg Books is an imprint of John Hunt Publishing Ltd., Laurel House, Station Approach,
Alresford, Hants, SO24 9JH, UK
office1@jhpbooks.net
www.johnhuntpublishing.com

For distributor details and how to order please visit the 'Ordering' section on our website.

ISBN: 978 1 78535 167 9
Library of Congress Control Number: 2015941037

A CIP catalogue record for this book is available from the British Library.

Design: Stuart Davies

Book cover designed by Ed Christiano at Deeper Blue Designs
www.db-md.co.uk

Printed and bound by CPI Group (UK) Ltd, Croydon, CR0 4YY, UK

We operate a distinctive and ethical publishing philosophy in all
areas of our business, from our global network of authors to
production and worldwide distribution.

CONTENTS

In memory of

Dorothy Soars
[1920 – 2014]

Margaret Roman
[1926 – 2014]

Sheila Greenwood
[1928 – 2000]

Tempus Fugit Semper Amici

For Mum.

My eternal inspiration and best friend.

1931-2015

Foreword

My fascination with the Oxfordshire version of the Mistletoe Bride legend was first ignited by my paternal grandmother, Florence Emily Slattery (nee Phipps), as it was her favourite story and one she passed on to whomever would listen – the ghost of the young bride roaming the manor for eternity her favourite part. She came from an Oxford family and knew of the legend from childhood. The location had a personal resonance because of her courtship of my grandfather, John (Jack) Joseph Slattery, at the time of WW1, when they met in the ruins.

Minster Lovell is a small village just outside of Oxford near to the Brize Norton Air Force Base. If you walk through the Hamlet, past the Old Swan Inn and the Minster Mill Hotel, and timber framed thatched cottages, you come to St Kenhelm's Church that sits in the lush greenery of the Oxfordshire countryside. It feels like stepping back into another time – one far removed from the modern world. If you then venture through the very atmospheric graveyard to the far side, it opens out onto fields with the river Windrush in the distance, and in the foreground you will be confronted with the ruins of an old manor house dating back to Lord Lovell, a loyal friend of King Richard III. It seems that when Richard was defeated in battle by Henry Tudor, who took the English crown as a result, Lord Lovell's lands were confiscated and the manor destroyed on the orders of the new King.

The original legend for the Mistletoe Bride was set in that pre-Tudor, medieval time and happened in what are now the remains of Lord Lovell's old manor at Minster Lovell. I made the decision to update it to Victorian England in 1893, simply because it was a time when the legend fascinated anew the Victorians, and indeed the poem about the tragedy was set to music by Thomas Haynes Bayley during this late Victorian period and titled The Mistletoe Bough!

When he suffered an injury during the Gallipoli campaign in WW1, my grandfather was returned to England to recover. This was when he met my grandmother and they started courting – she was a nurse at a nearby house, converted to a hospital for the army. They would stroll to Minster Lovell as part of their courtship, and his recuperation no doubt, and even carved their initials in the stones as lovers visiting the spot often did back then. He returned to the army and fought in France and survived the war. They married in 1920 and lived their entire life at Henley Avenue near Rose Hill, Oxford. They are buried in the cemetery at Rose Hill, together with my father and his brother.

This book is for them.

David Slattery-Christy

John Joseph Slattery & Florence Emily Slattery
(nee Phipps)
Oxford - Circa. 1920

Special Thanks to all of the following

My agent Robert Smith for his continued encouragement and support; Jane Cross and Anna Siminchenko for helping with Russian translations; Julie Craven for information regarding trans-mediums. Lesley Yalcin; Graham Greenwood; Ellen Aveyard; Nick Gaze for taking me to the ruins at Minster Lovell for the first time; Ed Christiano, Deeper Blue Designs for a brilliant cover design; The Randolph Hotel, Oxford; Lynn Nortcliff; Nicki Casey; Paul Taylor; Raymond Langford-Jones; Sheelagh Christophus; Grant Nightingale; John Hunt Publishers; David Brown and Michael Harvey. My editor Krystina Kellingley for her guidance, patience and encouragement.

The images used to depict Lady Ellen Forsyth for this book are those of Grace Lane a Victorian / Edwardian actress, who for me, captured the innocence and beauty of the character. I cast her posthumously in the role of the Mistletoe Bride and hope she would have approved.

Present Day

Willow Manor – Minster Lovell – Oxford

The roar came suddenly, as it always did, taking me by surprise and screeching hideously like some deranged demon in search of a soul to posses – maybe this time mine. I looked up through the tree cover but the low cloud obscured the view, this was of little consolation as I had seen it many times before, in my mind's eye it materialized all too vividly; even the December tree branches, bereft of their leaves, appeared to assume a sinister grasping role at the command of that sonorously voiced beast. I moved swiftly and ever soundlessly through a clump of trees, toward the gatehouse, terrified that this time it would find me. Even in my darkest and most lonely moments, my imagination had failed to enlighten me as to its evil capabilities.

At last, I had reached my destination. The huge wrought iron gates with the rusted and now deformed remains of my family crest loomed above me, an ominous swathe of interwoven chains kept them secured; the attached padlocks long since decayed and rust eaten, never to be opened again. A sudden flash of memory startled me with its clarity, and I could see them again as once they were – proud and welcoming wings at the portal of my beloved home. How long ago? I don't know. Time, as everything else, now seemed somehow meaningless.

I do remember how the gatehouse had been a hive of activity. Philips, the gateman, had been a loyal family servant from before I was even born. His twinkling blue eyes and strange lurching gait, the result of a riding accident in his youth, which, surprisingly, did nothing to impede his bright manner and easy humour.

His laughter would tinkle like fresh spring water, dancing over smooth pebbles in the meadow's brook. Strange how I remember such details, especially ones that seemed so insignificant at the time.

Looking around me, I could see too plainly how derelict the gatehouse had become – smashed windows; doors hanging off; full of filth and neglect which I could hardly bear to witness – a sad reflection of the manor beyond. Through the gates I could spy the very tips of the beautiful soaring spires of Oxford – how I longed to escape to them, to see them in their full glory once again. But, alas, I couldn't! Many times I had tried to leave but something held me back, although I know not what. I am trapped within the Manor and grounds, alone.

The demon had passed, its roar abated. Silently I walked back along the driveway accompanied by a frosty, whispering breeze. Tree roots, gnarled and ugly, had relentlessly pushed their way up through the once abundant and smooth shingled surface. I could almost hear the echoed sounds of long past Victoria carriages and horses serenely gliding along, the muffled crunch of gravel under wheel and hoof. Their journey would not be so simple now. Even the late afternoon mists that swirled around, so common to the Oxfordshire countryside, failed, as they sometimes did, to disguise the dilapidated state of the once meticulous and manicured drive and gardens.

As I turned with the vast sweeping of the drive, the Manor came into view. The once proud facade of that endlessly rambling house was covered in destructive ivy creepers, eating into it cancerously without the slightest compassion. I remember well how such an outcome had been predicted, and how the staff had fought endlessly to eradicate it, to protect the smooth cream sandstone – although I never dreamed that I would still be here to witness it. The countless windows stared down at me like dead black eyes, slithering green and black stains streaked down from its haughty sills and lintels, damp dripping and glistening like silent tears.

By thought alone, I was back in front of the main entrance and glad to be returning to the safety of the house. It was then I saw it, growing ethereally from the branches of an oak tree – Mistletoe! My long-past wedding day rushed to my mind's eye. My once beautiful wedding dress now rotted by mould and as decayed as my spirit. The rush of pain and sadness enveloped me instantly; suffocating me. I cried out: "Are you there?" I then swung round but only at some imagined noise. "Is that you, Lovell? I have waited, as I knew you would come. You have come for me haven't you?" The silence was shattering. I will wait patiently as I always have…one day he will come…I know he will…someone must!"

* * *

At the nearby Brize Norton air-force base, the fighter jet was approaching to land. Nicholai Roman, the pilot, was adjusting the controls and wondering about the abandoned manor house he flew over regularly on this flight path. Who did it belong to? Why was it abandoned and derelict? He made up his mind he would go and explore the grounds and house and satisfy his curiosity once and for all. Something about the place intrigued him. Smiling to himself, he was rudely jolted back to the job at hand by air-traffic control, as they gave him permission to land. The jet's engines gave a final roar as he hit the runway and then burst into reverse thrust.

Chapter 1

The Beginning After the End – Present Day

My story has taken an intolerable time to find a resolution. Breaking the surface at last has enabled me to share with you the convolutions of fate that has brought me to this present day. I have a voice again. My heart aches with the longing, innocence, devastation and interminable loneliness that accompanied me through my short life and then forward to this time. A time that is incomprehensible to me, and a time I was never meant to see if the normal rules of living had applied to me. For more than one hundred and twenty years I have longed to be able to rest – to find peace – and, as importantly, put right the terrible wrong done to me and also to those I loved. Wickedness beyond my comprehension was at the root of everything.

Forgive me. I need to start at the beginning to enable you to understand. It seems so long ago and the memory of a time when the surge of happiness and joy I experienced, as a young woman about to marry the man I loved, envelopes me still when I think of it. Everything was ahead of me – or so I thought. Fate, I know only too well, had other ideas, other plans, and other paths to thrust me along. This is no time for tears. Tears are no use now, and never were they except as an accompaniment to pointless self-pity. The only thing I ask is that you reserve judgement until the story is complete – however hard that may be at times. I would love to suck in life giving lungs of fresh, sweet air – as one does to inspire courage at a time when determination is needed.

My name is Ellen, Lady Ellen Forsyth of Willow Manor, Oxfordshire. As much as I was married for a few short hours, I continue to refer to myself by my maiden name. My marriage was never consummated, so therefore I feel unmarried but also because I never knew a life of marriage with my darling, Lord Lovell. Time for me is now limited – not much left before I have to move on to that other place, a blessed place where the spirit soars once the ties to this mortal plane are untethered. To proceed with my story, for the sake of clarity, I must take you back, back to 1893 a few days before Christmas and my ill-fated wedding.

Father was beside himself at the prospect of my nuptials, by Christmas Eve morning he was so excited as to be rather irritating to some but amusing for me to behold. He had been counting the days and driving the staff demented with various demands about the wedding plans and the invitation list, at all hours of the day and night. As a result the command bells tinkled constantly in the servant's hall, so much so I had to speak to him firmly because I worried for his health over his erratic behaviour – not to mention the effect of this on the servants' moral. However, secretly, I was pleased for him, simply because it was the first time for a long time I had seen that mischievous glint in his eye again – so often there before Mother died suddenly and tragically young. Charlotte, my only sister, and I were barely out of the nursery when Mother died. I feel it more keenly than Charlotte, perhaps because I am named after her.

Mother and my father, so he told me many times, had given a wonderful dinner party and had danced all night to the popular waltzes in the ballroom. They were devoted and always in love and a sight to behold in admiration and awe among those fortunate to witness them. I had always dreamed of finding a love like theirs with a special someone. A love that accepts silence as comfortable, and finds no demands or obligation to constantly entertain or amuse. A love where a brief look or a suggestion of a smile can convey more than a thousand words spoken ever could. My parents were my example for defining love.

After that dazzling ball my mother and father had gone to bed as normal, delighted that everything had gone so well and the company had enjoyed their hospitality. Happy, but exhausted,

Mother had fallen asleep never to wake again. Her heart just stopped, for no reason her doctors could explain. The shock for my father to awaken and feel my mother's cold body in his embrace was horrifying and the memory of it became unbearable. He raged at God and fate that his darling wife should be torn from his side in such a cruel and heartless way. My father was never the same man after that. Nothing consoled him for his loss. His soul mate had gone and nothing would ever be the same.

He wore his loneliness and heartbreak like a shroud. He was never a man with great ambition or interest in politics, shooting, hunting or estate management as were many of his contemporaries. He led a fairly simple but privileged life at Willow Manor. He had been an only child and heir for his parents – parents who were odd strangers to him because he was born to them when they were older than conventional parents. They were out of tune and out of time with each other. He inherited the manor and title of Baron Forsyth of Littlemore whilst still up at Oxford, when they died suddenly within days of each other. They lay in the family crypt, he would say, as cold to each other in death as they had been in life.

His formative years as a border at Eton made his parents somehow strangers, which is perhaps why he sought to find a love that was warm and real and enduring. In my mother, Ellen, herself from a low status Oxford family, he had found his ideal. He cared not a jot for social conformity and it took time for Mother to be accepted by the local families and in society in general. However, my mother was secretly admired for her beauty, determination and grace. Many a time she was the object of deliciously whispered gossip and scandal at society balls and dinner parties.

Father was immensely proud of her achievements as a hostess and that she had even caught the attention of Bertie, the Prince of Wales. Renowned for seducing beautiful women who took his fancy, she was for a short time in his sights. She flattered him but made it clear that friendship was all that was on offer – this made him roar with laughter and respect her even more for not being afraid to refuse him. His Royal Highness, noted for taking a delight in mischief making among society snobs, deliberately invited himself for a weekend at Willow Manor, so Mother could throw a grand ball in his honour that would once and for all silence her critics and make her the most sought after guest on the invitation lists of Oxford and London society events from that point on.

It continued the royal connection to our family and the manor. Father's family had been granted the land that Willow Manor was built on by King Charles II. His father King Charles I had used Oxford as his capital city during the civil war. Sought by Cromwell's troops, the King had hidden in property owned by Father's ancestors, the Forsyth's, in Hinksey Village, near old Botley, on the outskirts of Oxford. They remained loyal to the King and at his defeat, several of Father's ancestors had their land and properties confiscated and were executed for their association with him – considered as treasonable by the Roundheads. Once the monarchy was restored and Charles II took the throne, he gifted the land to the family and ennobled them with a Baronetcy for their loyalty. The hereditary title continued to my father's day. He had two daughters, so was hoping one of us would bear a son and heir for the title to continue. That, as you will discover, was another loss for the family. He little realized it at the time, but my father turned out to be the last Baron Littlemore.

Charlotte, my sister, seemed to have inherited some of the cold aloofness, in public at least, that was typical of Father's parents. But to me she was always warm and generous and an object of my intense admiration. When Mother died she was little more than ten years old but she immediately took on the role of mother to me, her younger sister by more than four years. She made me feel safe and would always defend me, even against Father's rages that erupted in the early years after Mother's death. These rages, so out of character for my father, I later understood to be the result of loneliness, drink and grief. Only now do I realize the terrible burden placed upon Charlotte's young shoulders at that time.

To me she is quite beautiful but always she has felt inferior to me in that regard – a nonsense I tell her whenever the issue is raised in moments of silly, sisterly arguments. Indeed I once asked Father not to keep suggesting that my beauty, so like my dear departed mother's, was so superior to that of Charlotte's, whose features were "strong and practical" by comparison. I could see the pain behind Charlotte's eyes when these opinions were voiced so nonchalantly. She would never show outwardly how hurtful she found such comments – but I knew it penetrated as deeply as a knife wound.

I was in awe of Charlotte's capabilities, intelligence and wisdom. She was a shrewd and capable manager of people and able to organize, a brilliant communicator, a talent she exercised frequently on the servants, but had little else beyond the house and estate to which she could deploy those skills. She may have been a woman, but her abilities matched those of any man and surpassed even Father, who found the duties of running such a large manor and estate tiresome and an increasing burden financially.

The colour of our eyes was the only thing Charlotte openly envied. She had inherited the deep brown, a throwback from Father's side of the family, whereas I had the pale, striking blue of my father and mother's. Other than that, aside from her irritability at times, again a trait of Father's, she was a perfect older sister. She was as excited as I was at my forthcoming wedding, or so I believed, but I did wonder if she felt that, as the elder, it should have been her right to marry first. If she felt that, she never said as much at the time. However, now I know the full story, I understand things from a different perspective. I cannot believe I could have been so blind and ignorant of so much that was going on.

Florence, the housekeeper at Willow Manor for years, had also been an important part of our lives and someone who Father came to rely on more and more after Mother's death. Florence had become a steadying force for my father when he was torn apart with grief. She kept the house in order and made sure the servants and estate staff continued to work efficiently and appropriately. Her uncle, Phillips, and his small family, lived in the gatehouse at the entrance to the estate. He was the perfect sentinel and was fierce in his loyalty and duties as gateman. He had started working for Father as a stable boy many years before and worked his way up to head groom. He then had a terrible accident, being thrown from a frisky stallion he was trying to break, and it damaged his leg. Once he recovered he realized rather quickly that he would be unable to walk properly again or continue doing his duties. He gave notice to leave but Father would not hear of it. He moved him and his family into the gatehouse, where he created a position for him as gatekeeper, this secured his status among the estate servants and also made sure he could continue to provide for his family.

In time, Florence became a mentor to Charlotte and myself and in some ways even a surrogate mother. She did that rare thing in aristocratic houses; she crossed the line between servant and master. To me she was, and always would be, family. To my father she was irreplaceable on many levels and they did establish a strange friendship of sorts that relieved the pressure for him, as Florence took on more and more of the duties Mother had done so well in the house and on the estate. All this was carried out under a veil of respectability, and no guest or caller to Willow Manor would have guessed at what they would have considered at the very least impropriety, and at worst less than respectable. Charlotte was the official family and public face for the smooth running of the house, after Father. No matter. We were, in our own rather oddly eccentric way, happy and content with the status quo.

The day that Lovell was arriving with his best man, the Russian Count, Nicholai Romanov, had dawned. This was eagerly anticipated and had caused us all much excitement I remember. Florence, Charlotte and I were in my bedroom suite. I was having a fitting for my wedding gown. I was standing rather precariously on a footstool in my elaborate dress, made from ivory silk, with intricate pearling and beading work on the boned bodice. It was far from finished though. Mrs. Drummond, the dressmaker was making adjustments to the hem, helped by our housemaid, Millie.

As I recall, Charlotte had grown tired of fussing about the dress, she never had much patience for dressmaking and fittings, and had been standing looking out of the window for some time – her own impenetrable thoughts had got the better of her. We were well used to her interminable silences and occasional sulks. There was a side to my sister that then I had not really under-stood or even suspected. Perhaps I was oblivious to it because I didn't want to believe she was anything but a perfect sibling.

The story as it happened needs to speak for itself. I must not interfere with it for my sake, or in response to my emotional reaction because it is newly revealed to me, I have to enable you an impartial perspective, I need to allow that to happen as we progress.

Florence above everyone, I now see, had become aware that Charlotte could at times behave strangely and in a way that worried her intensely. She made allowances, as did most of us, because Charlotte had had to shoulder so much responsibility, at so young an age, on the death of Mother. Shortly before my wedding, Father had commissioned a portrait to be painted of me as a Mistletoe Bride. My mother had also been his Mistletoe Bride, and in his way he was honouring her memory and also marking the occasion of my marriage to Lord Lovell. The portrait had been completed and hung in the drawing room and covered with a silk cloth so as not to create bad luck for me – seeing the bride in her dress before the wedding was tempting fate. How ironic that statement is, knowing what I know now and everything that has happened since! (If I could laugh at such irony, it would be nothing but a discordant, hollow sound that would abruptly turn into racking sobs of despair and anger.) However, Father was adamant that nobody could see the portrait until after my marriage, in Willow Manor's private family chapel on Christmas Eve 1893.

What is a Mistletoe Bride? It is an old tradition that no longer applies or has any meaning, and perhaps even in my time its relevance was diminishing. It is simple to explain. When one gets married on Christmas Eve, it is traditional to be a Mistletoe Bride. It has its roots in old English pagan traditions but in the Victorian era it was the decorative and sentimental elements that persisted. To have a bride's headdress and floral handheld display using mistletoe, made the most of seasonal plants and added an element of Christmas to the ceremony – not forgetting the ancient fertility meaning behind the mistletoe sprigs! The darker side of mistletoe escaped me at the time. It is a parasite that feeds off another living thing to be able live and thrive itself. How dark and twisted that seems now after everything that has happened. The night before my dress fitting, unbeknown to me at the time, there had been a strange nocturnal dispute between my sister and Florence.

In the dead of night Charlotte had lit her bedside candle and listened for any sounds of family or servants still moving about the house. The silence and stillness of the night reassured her that everyone was asleep. As quietly as she could she pushed aside her bed covers, swung her legs to the floor and slipped her feet into her slippers. Again she listened intently. She moved slowly and steadily towards the bedroom door, protecting the flickering candle flame with her cupped hand. The sound of a distant dog barking somewhere on the estate brought her to an abrupt halt. She composed herself and slowly opened her door and walked along the deeply carpeted landing. Her footsteps were inaudible as she passed swiftly by the painted portraits of ancestors and their wives and children. The candle light flickering gave them an eerie, haunting scowl and Charlotte could no doubt see their disapproving, beady eyes as she walked quickly by. Once she reached the landing to the grand staircase, she stopped and collected her breath, at the same time listening for any sounds of life. The ticking of the huge grandfather clock at the foot of the stairs seemed to echo through the vast hallway and staircase. It began to chime and then struck the hour of 3:00am. The flickering candle flame reflected brilliantly on the highly polished mahogany banister of the curving staircase, and glinted here and there in the crystals of the huge unlit chandelier. She glided silently down the stairs as if floating on some ethereal mist. Unbeknown to Charlotte, Florence was watching her progress from behind a marbled pillar, on the opposite side of the upper landing. She had been doing her final rounds and locking up for the night when she had seen the flickering light and had hidden in anticipation of seeing an intruder – or an errant servant up to no good. She even wondered if the Baron was still awake and wandering, as he had done often when newly bereaved all those years ago.

Charlotte crossed the hallway and entered the drawing room and slowly closed the door nearly shut to avoid any noise. She again listened intently for signs she had been discovered and then walked to the French doors leading to the garden. Suddenly, and despite the coolness of the room and season, she found herself feeling rather hot and had a desire for fresh air. Perhaps her nocturnal secrecy had made her heart pump faster and that explained her warm, unpleasant flush of perspiration. She placed the candle on the side table and slowly unlocked the door with a click. It sounded like a gunshot in the quiet stillness of the night. She held her breath in case anyone had heard and footsteps began to approach. Silence. She let out a sigh in relief and then opened the door to feel the cold December air rush over her and she instinctively gulped in a deep breath that also cooled her down. The candle flame began to flicker erratically and she slowly closed the French door lest it be extinguished. As she did, she caught a reflection of herself in the mirror opposite and for a moment it didn't feel as if it was her own image looking back at her. The reflection seemed odd and distorted to her eyes. She shivered and held her own gaze in the mirror until she was sure there was no phantom spying on her activities.

Florence was observing through the slightly ajar door and decided that Charlotte was up to some mischief. As she watched she thought about the hurt that inside boiled away at her because I was marrying before her. Poor Charlotte had never had a chance to be social because she had been the one Father had decided should look after him and be the family face of house and estate. As much as this was unfair, it was the way it was. She was also not the beauty that I had become, added to the fact that I was the image of Mother – almost a living incarnation. How could Charlotte ever compete with that? Florence worried about Charlotte and her future. There was a darkness in Charlotte's eyes sometimes that shocked her. She had to keep a close protective watch over her. Charlotte crossed the room, picked up the candle and moved towards the fireplace. It was at this point that Florence knew what she was about to do.

Charlotte moved almost in a trance towards the fireplace, staring at the fine, silk sheet that covered the enormous portrait above. The silk was moving and rippling with the residue of the air that had burst through the open French window. It was as if it taunted her somehow, teased her with the prospect of what lay beneath. She only wanted to see it for herself, so the shock of seeing it with others, looking at her for her reaction to my portrait, would be manageable, and they wouldn't be able to judge her expression. The candle flickered as she held her other hand up to grasp the corner of the shimmering silk cloth. Gently, taking the corner and holding the softness of the silk in her fingers, she gave it a slight tug. For a second or two nothing happened. Then, like a rushing ripple on a millpond, the silk fluttered down and settled with a whisper by her feet. She hesitated for a moment before looking up to see the portrait of me in my wedding dress – a Mistletoe Bride. It was uncanny how much I looked like Mother. A tear pricked the corner of her eye and she swiped it away angrily with the back of her free hand. A sob suddenly escaped from her throat – a clump of pain that had to get out as quickly as possible. "My dear sister, Ellen," she had whispered to the portrait, a sinister edge to her voice, "You may be more beautiful than I, but where is my happiness?" My heart aches at this revelation – I never knew in life she felt like that about me.

"Charlotte!" demanded Florence in a hissing whisper. "What on earth are you doing wandering about the house at this time of night?" The French door suddenly crashed open with a gust of wind that blew the candle out. Startled, but recovering herself quickly, she added, "Why have you disobeyed your father's wishes." She pointed to the portrait. "He will be furious if he finds out about this."

Florence rushed over to close and lock the French doors; afraid the noise would disturb the house. She then relit the candle and her eyes met Charlotte's defiantly for a few moments. Charlotte broke the gaze and bent down to gather up the silk at her feet and handed it to Florence.

"Please, Florence," her voice and demeanour now sweet and charming, "don't tell Father. I just had to see it tonight. Isn't it beautiful? Please, promise me you won't tell Father? I don't want to spoil his surprise."

Florence looked at her and wondered at the sudden changes

in her mood and character. She switched between two distinct personalities. One so loving and kind and the other with eyes like the very devil. "Off to bed with you now and I will think about it," she said, adding a tone to her whispering voice that Charlotte could recognise instantly as a signal that conversation was at an end. "And don't let me catch you creeping about the house in the dead of night again. You could fall and hurt yourself."

Charlotte knew then that Florence would tell nobody about this, certainly not Father. "Thank you, darling Florence," her tone almost mocking. She then kissed her cheek lightly. "I do love you dearly."

Florence watched her as she glided out of the doorway and up the sweeping staircase, leaving her in the gloom of the room. She became aware of the moonlight escaping from behind the night sky's scudding clouds. "There is something not right with that girl," she said to herself. "Girl?" It then occurred to Florence that she still referred to us as girls, but in fact we were both young women. Charlotte was 28 years old!

"Ouch! That hurt!" Mrs Drummond and Millie appeared from under the skirts of my wedding dress with a mouth full of stickpins that she hastily removed before uttering an apology of sorts. "Please be more careful, I am tired of being a pincushion, that's all." My legs were aching and my shoulders were stiff with having to stand so erect and still for so long.

"Yes, my lady. Sorry my lady," she replied with sincerity before diving beneath my skirts, to continue her mysterious adjustments, that seemed to me pointless, as the skirt hung beautifully. The intricately embroidered sprigs of mistletoe shone and caught my eye. I marvelled at the patience the seamstress had shown using the fine, silk threads. The thought calmed my mind, I remember, and a surge of emotion made me feel suddenly weepy.

"Patience now, Lady Ellen," interjected Florence with her

usual kindness and calming manner. "She is only doing her job and we want things to be perfect don't we?" She smiled brightly before looking over towards Charlotte, who stood gazing from the window indifferent to my plight with the dressmaking pins.

Out in the Oxfordshire country side, whilst this was going on, on route to Willow Manor, Lovell and his friend, the Russian Count, Nicholai Andreovitch Romanov, cousin to the Tsar, and soon to be best man at Lovell's and my wedding, were enduring a rather bumpy and uncomfortable journey from Oxford in a Victoria carriage pulled by four horses. The atmosphere was as chilly in the carriage as the bleak but beautiful countryside it hurtled past, with thundering, galloping hoofs and the crunch of the wheels on the rough country lanes. The silence was beginning to become somewhat uncomfortable as Nicholai smiled and tried to put Lovell at ease. They had started arguing almost immediately the carriage had pulled away from the Randolph Hotel and headed along St Giles to the Woodstock Road and out towards Lovell Minster.

Nicholai was a handsome Russian. His dark, swarthy looks complimented by a neat beard of dark, lush hair to match the naturally waved hair on his head. His beard would come and go, Lovell told me, depending on his mood and how much it irritated him. His eyes were a dark green, punctuated by the longest eyelashes ever seen on any man. His nose was perfectly proportioned and his high cheekbones all added something to the overall handsomeness he possessed. His physique was sturdy and strong, standing at over five feet ten inches, he seemed even taller somehow, his limbs perfectly proportioned to his torso. In his right eye he had a small brown fleck, like a beauty spot, but in the white of his eye. It caused him no inconvenience or problems with his vision. It was just an anomaly developed in the womb. It was fascinating and marked him out as different. He had perfect English but, apart from his native Russian, he could speak several other languages quite fluently.

Lord Lovell, my intended, on the other hand was naturally fair of hair and had very deep blue eyes that seemed to vary in depth of colour and intensity depending on his temper and health. He was not as handsome as his friend, Nicholai, but his features were striking and well proportioned. He cultivated a moustache and well-manicured beard that were of his own invention and certainly didn't conform to current fashion. He was an inch shorter than his friend but just as sturdy in terms of physique. His hands were strong and his nails beautifully manicured. The fair hair that covered his forearms and wrists always tantalisingly visible at the line of his cuffs – this added to his masculinity and was certainly attractive and appealing.

As their bumpy journey progressed, Nicholai had asked Lovell if this hamlet of Minster Lovell was anything to do with his family. Lovell had told him some of the history. His ancestor, another Lord Lovell, had been a rather unsavoury character and loyal henchman to the infamous Yorkist King, Richard III. His association and loyalty to Richard had provided great wealth and power and he had built a large manor house at Lovell Minster that now lay in ruins. After the King's death and the rise of the Tudor King Henry, his lands were confiscated and the manor destroyed. Lovell fled and was assumed to be dead on the same battlefield as King Richard. Ironically, Willow Manor is built on lands that would have once belonged to his ancestor – not that far from the ghostly ruins of the ancient manor at Lovell Minster.

Lovell and Nicholai had met as undergraduates at Oxford, and their college, Brasenose, was where fate thrust them together. On arriving and being allocated rooms for their first term, they were both decidedly reluctant to accept a shared set of rooms instead of the hoped for single accommodations. Their protestations to the college warden and tutors had been in vain and nothing else could be arranged. It was that or nothing, or one of them would have to agree to move out. Neither was prepared to compromise in that direction. With reluctance they accepted the situation and after a few days they began to form what would soon become a bond of friendship that would last a lifetime. A characteristic of their developing friendship was Nicholai's habit of cursing in Russian whenever he didn't get his own way or didn't agree with a current topic or argument they were engaged in. Lovell, at such times, would refuse to speak to Nicholai until he switched back to English. As years passed they spent more and more time together until they became inseparable. Indeed, they would share rooms at Oxford for the entire three years, until they both left to embark on their respective careers – Nicholai in the Russian Navy, assigned to the Tsar's personal yacht, the Standart. Lovell would carve out a career for himself in the Royal Navy and then at the War Office as an attaché. Neither of them had any real family to speak of, so their bond was closer than would be usual for that time for two young men.

As the carriage wheels hurtled over a mound in the road, then lurched and its occupants were nearly thrown into the air, adding to their discomfort, Nicholai let out an expletive in Russian under his breath. Lovell smiled to himself and then heard Nicholai curse again.

"Forgive me." Nicholai smiled and adjusted his position to try and make himself more comfortable. "I only meant to say it was rather..."

Lovell looked at him and cut him off with a smile. "Stuffy?" Amused at Nicholai's shock that he had understood his Russian he pulled the leather strap to lower the window. The cold air gushed into the carriage bringing with it an invigorating freshness that had an immediate effect on both of them. "My Russian is not so bad after all these years. I have no aptitude for languages, as you know, Nicholai – but certain words I recognize occasionally. Did you enjoy staying at the Randolph?

"Preferable to those dismal, damp rooms we once shared at Brasenose, as I recall," replied Nicholai with a hint of sarcasm.

"I forget how mild the English winters seem to you. Is it

terribly cold in St Petersburg?

"You should have made the effort to come to my home for yourself and find out." Nicholai eyed Lovell and then added with sarcasm, "How many years have you been promising to do just that?"

"I have been so occupied since we left Oxford. The Navy and then the War Office have taken over my life." He looked at Nicholai's handsome profile whilst admiring the view, and then added sincerely, "It is good to see you again after so long, Nicholai."

Nicholai was silent for the longest time and then rather wistfully replied without looking at his friend, "Yes, a few years have passed – a long time – I have missed our friendship." He turned to look directly at Lovell and then smiled brightly. Lovell suddenly became uncomfortable under Nicholai's intense gaze.

"A day has not passed when I haven't," he hesitated as if he was struggling to find the right words to express himself, "haven't thought of you." After a silence where they both stared out the window, followed by another abrupt lurch of the carriage that launched them into the air, Lovell added, "I appreciated all your letters."

"Indeed." He stared as Lovell made himself comfortable again. "And now I am to witness your marriage as your friend and best man."

"Maybe Ellen and I can travel to Russia after we are married? You could give us the grand tour…"

Nicholai's reply was anything but enthusiastic. "As you wish, Lovell."

There was an odd sense of sadness between them as the carriage rocked and jolted its way along the rough country lanes. The trees and landscape had been frosted by the cold December weather and the beauty of the mist-laden landscape became more apparent as their journey progressed. Willow Manor came into view on the far horizon. It looked impressive as always – even from this distant vantage point. It teased the eye as to what majesty it would reveal on closer inspection, as it became ever nearer and more magnificent.

"Look, there it is!" exclaimed an excited Lovell. This did nothing to ease Nicholai's sense of dread and irritation at his friend. "Oh, Nicholai, you'll love Willow Manor and you will adore Ellen and her family too. They are all charming and can't wait to meet you."

Nicholai seemed less than delighted at this exuberant boyishness and the obvious happiness in Lovell's voice. "It will be my pleasure, it is why I am here after all," he said, whilst looking intently at Lovell, who was looking off into the distance with an expression of expectation on his face that Nicholai found almost unbearable – as if it was a physical pain for him. "You still haven't told me why you cancelled our planned meeting three months ago. I thought you enjoyed dinner parties and would have wanted to see me after such a long time?"

Lovell looked at him to judge if he was angry or just teasing him. "You were only in London for a week and I was here with Ellen. I knew there would be another time for us soon. And I was right – here you are – and I am grateful you accepted my request to be my best man."

"Let's not talk about it now," Nicholai said impatiently, "I don't want to fight with you again today." He shuddered and then slid the window closed as the carriage had become cold. The sudden silence added to the heavy atmosphere between them.

They rounded the corner and the huge ornamental gates came into view. Phillips, the gate-man was standing watching as they approached. The gates were open and he waved them through. Nicholai watched the horses as great gushing plumes of their hot breath was expelled from flaring nostrils at gasping, snorting speed. The sleek, powerful and sweaty horses trotted through the gates of Willow Manor, straining as their muscles twitched and ached to gallop on unrestrained. The power of these animals lurched the carriage forward as it made its approach along the manicured driveway.

Nicholai was transfixed with the seeming perfect exterior of Willow Manor and its grounds as it moved into close view. The Manor itself seemed an endless rambling house constructed of rich, creamy, Cotswold stone. The windows were of Georgian proportions making the reception rooms, he imagined, bright and airy, if perhaps somewhat cold at this time of year. But there were many fireplaces to counteract that – the impressive roof chimneys testament to their existence. As such, Nicholai was not surprised to see trails of smoke curling up into the still, cold, Oxfordshire air. The gardens that he could see were immaculate and reflected the number of servants obviously employed on the estate to ensure that the grounds were well maintained and manicured. Should I, Lovell's bride, be as perfect at sight, he thought with a sneer, he would not be at all surprised. The English and their imperiousness and straight-laced, prudish attitude to life were intolerable. He then became aware of Lovell looking at him with concern etched across his face. Nicholai smiled at him reassuringly – glad Lovell was unable to read his immediate thoughts. It would seem I was not as accepted and liked by him as I then believed.

"You are determined to proceed," he asked Lovell with kindness in his voice for the first time, "to proceed with this marriage?"

Lovell responded to the warmth in Nicholai's voice. "I do love Ellen," he said, "and we shall be very happy together."

"As your friend – my concern is only for you." He looked at Lovell and smiled reassuringly. "It is not too late to change your mind."

Lovell immediately felt uncomfortable and defensive. "No, please, Nicholai, don't! Ellen and I are honoured that you agreed to be here for me – for us – please just try and be happy for us."

Lovell turned his attention to the staff waiting at the entrance of Willow Manor as the they shuddered to a halt. Nicholai looked out and caught the movement of an upstairs curtain. He looked up to see Charlotte standing in the window looking down at him. As their eyes locked, they were both shocked to see each other. They had met before that day. Nicholai broke the gaze and began to exit the carriage. From the corner of his eye, as he walked across to the entrance portico, he could still feel her eyes upon him. The footmen were busy collecting the luggage as Lovell led him into the house to be greeted by my father, the Baron Forsyth of Littlemore.

Charlotte was shaken. She couldn't believe whom she had just seen. She immediately began to plan her response to this man coming into her life again so unexpectedly – and in such intimate family setting and at her sister's wedding. She had had no idea that he was also the famous, charming and brilliant Nicholai of Lovell's friendship. Perhaps it could all work to her advantage, she thought. She then determined how to work out the best way to handle this.

"Oh, Millie, please close your mouth and stop gawping!" I exclaimed in increasingly frustrated tones, oblivious at the time to what had happened, "Have you never seen a wedding dress before?"

Millie looked slightly crestfallen and her face coloured a deep red. "It just looks so…" she struggled to find the right word as we all wait for her to finish, "beautiful."

"Well it doesn't feel very beautiful," I snapped, "at this moment it feels so heavy…"

Florence was listening to all this with good humour but realized that time was running out and they needed to get a move on with the alterations.

"Come along, Millie! The procession is tomorrow tonight, the wedding the day after, and it is hoped that Lady Ellen will be wearing this dress – if it's ever finished."

"Yes, Miss Florence, I'm sorry..." Millie began to finish pinning the bodice of the dress.

I sighed with resignation and then looked for Charlotte – who was still standing by the window. "Charlotte, are you determined to spend all day looking out of that window?"

"Didn't you hear the carriage, Ellen," interjected Florence, "probably your aunt, Lady Marlborough, arriving with her usual vigour?"

"Charlotte – is it our aunt?" I asked becoming more irritated by her indifference.

Charlotte turned to us and crossed the room. "Don't worry, Ellen, it isn't our beloved, demon aunt arriving." She paused to make the most of the news she was about to impart to us. "Just Lovell and Count Romanov."

"Why didn't you say so, Charlotte!" I jumped down from the stool and I tried to unhook the dress. "Get me out of this dress now – I need to go and greet our guests, Father will expect it of me." Mrs Drummond, Millie and Florence struggled to get me out of the dress. "Charlotte, you are infuriating at times."

As I wriggled to free myself from the cumbersome dress, Charlotte turned to leave the room with a satisfied smirk on her face. Florence observed it all and, as usual, ended up worrying where this would all lead.

Chapter 2

A New Incarnation – A New Time – Present Day

The heavenly view of my abandoned home, Willow Manor, I could not imagine, but it had always fascinated Nicholai. Every time he came in to land at Brize Norton Air Base, he found his attention drawn to our rambling, old, stately home. He little realized that I was there watching, and exhausted in my fear to escape him and his infernal machine. He had always promised himself that one day he would come and see it from the ground. That day was now drawing ever closer. It never ceased to amaze him, in his private thoughts, how the English could leave a place so beautiful, so near the enchanting city of Oxford with all its history, to decay and crumble away. Nicholai didn't understand, as I did, that actually it would not be his first visit to Willow Manor. His first visit in this new life, but he had been there before – another lifetime ago. The roar of the jet's engines vibrated the air as they thundered into reverse thrust every time he touched down on the nearby runway. He had no idea I was still here at Willow Manor eagerly awaiting his eventual return.

As for Charlotte, she was also on a course to be reunited with her ancestral home. She might use the name Charley in this new life, but her damaged spirit was the same. In this life she could forge a path for herself that was forbidden way back then. All those skills I knew she possessed, she made good use of, working in what I have now discovered is called real estate and property development. But the darkness was still there in her eyes, the wickedness still casting a long, ugly shadow over her soul – a soul that had no regrets for her actions in this life or the last. I was also waiting for her to return to Willow Manor. Between them the present day Nicholai and Charley would bring to me the man who was the reason for my former happiness and my present haunted soul being trapped in this place, waiting for him to finally set me free. To seek revenge for the pain that had been wrought on my innocence, to eradicate the loss that I had endured, to make up for the lost time where we should all have lived full lives and flourished into old age with happiness. I always prayed Lovell would come back for me one day. Never realizing it would take so long. Now I have seen everything, I understand more about that world of the present and that fateful day they returned to the manor. It unravelled like this:

Charley knew she was late and as a result had decided to take a chance and exceed the speed limit in her horseless carriage. This was typical of her impetuous nature. The many laned road was quieter than normal and she guessed that it would be a different story in a few days, when Christmas Eve was upon the world. Besides, she enjoyed speeding, she often told herself aloud. Sometimes she found herself entranced and wanted to go faster and faster – even wondering sometimes what would happen if she just carried on and didn't apply the brakes. Just what would happen? Would she feel anything or would every-thing end in the microsecond of the collision? She shook herself and once again found herself wondering why she had such black thoughts. As she sped up to, and tailgated another driver, impatiently flashing her headlights until they moved out of her path, then zooming past and off towards Oxford, she saw the exit signs for Brize Norton. The car radio blared out Reflections, an old Diana Ross song.

Charley looked in the rear-view mirror, prior to approaching a bend in the lane, and suddenly she saw my face with staring eyes, wearing my tattered, mouldy bridal veil. She could even suddenly smell my vile odour of damp and decay in that split second I appeared to her. My veiled face contorted into a gasping, writhing creature as I clawed behind the reflection to get to her.

She swerved the wheel to regain control of the car, but I was able to make sure she could not move the wheel, and then a sharp bend was suddenly upon her. The front end of the car scraped along a hedge and the sound of twigs tearing over her car's paintwork seemed to signal she was out of control and would crash. She could barely bring herself to do it, but looked again in the mirror. She hastily turned the radio off. All she could see now was her own stricken face staring back at her, with beads of perspiration forming on her forehead. She manoeuvred the carriage off the grass verge and onto the side of the road, opened the window and took some deep breaths of the cold air. The smell of my decay filled the car and nauseated her as it had done to me for so long. She wondered if it must have been something she had eaten that had upset her system. Her handheld machine began to ring. She pressed a button and spoke to it, surprised to hear a slight shake in her own voice.

"Yes, yes. I am nearly there. I will make sure the signs are up today." She wiped the sweat from her brow with a tissue and checked her make up in the mirror. "Nicholai? Yes, I am on my way to the base now to pick him up. If he calls again tell him I am nearly there. Thanks."

She clicked off the contraption. She gazed into the rear view mirror again and was relieved to see just her own reflection. She struggled to bring to mind my face but decided it was so weird and so...what was the word she was looking for? It seemed odd to describe someone as looking pitiful but evil, she thought, but that was the best way she could - sad, pitiful and those piercing blue eyes. That is crazy; she thought instantly, how could she tell it had blue eyes? Charley felt an odd sensation again and a shiver went up her spine. She shrugged it off and turned the ignition, making the carriage roar into life with a throbbing sense of power. With the steering wheel between her hands, and in her control again, she immediately felt better. More like her old self.

Charley didn't know it then but it was when I knew it really was her. That she really was alive again. I knew she would be drawn back to Willow Manor in this new incarnation. It was, I realize now, the moment that I saw her again for the first time after nearly a century. Forgive me, but you must understand that as much as I was convinced it was her, she looked different and I needed to be certain it wasn't my mind playing tricks and I was seeing someone who just resembled Charlotte in this present world. In spite of this, I raged inside for I was the one "trapped in a world of distorted reality," I was the one who could now see "reflections of you and me" and what had happened in that past life we had shared. I could sense the strands of fate coming together. I felt sure that one day soon we would all be back together, that they would all have to come back to Willow Manor.

Charley's behaviour in this new life didn't surprise me at all. This was so typical of her and further evidence that little had been learned or understood in the years after my death in 1893, or with the opportunity to live another life in another time. The twists and turns of the country lanes did little to reduce her speed – indeed it added an edge of excitement for her as she narrowly avoided losing control again.

* * *

Nicholai had been satisfied with the test flight of the new European Fighter Jet and was looking forward to preparing a full report in the New Year, for the Ministry of Defence and his counterparts in Washington and NATO. He had returned to his quarters to shower and change in preparation for Charley's arrival; as they were due to spend Christmas together at the Randolph Hotel in Oxford. He had one last meeting with his commander, Air Marshall Forsyth. This man looked like my father but was not a direct reincarnation of him; his spirit was not the same. Although the easy relationship he had with present day Nicholai mirrored the past relationship with my father at the time of my wedding. Thankfully in this new life they were close colleagues, so they could happily have their meeting in Nicholai's quarters to save time. Nicholai was also seeing his niece in this life, Charley, whose arrival was imminent. They had obvious respect for each other and for the work they did for the Air Forces of their respective countries.

"So, Nicholai, how was Moscow?" said Forsyth, getting straight to the point as usual. "They can be tricky to deal with, the Russians."

Nicholai smiled. "Let me put it this way, sir. The exchange scheme was a great idea in theory, but the Russians are so paranoid where defence is concerned. Made worse by Putin and his recent escapades in the Crimea and Ukraine – what he sanctioned in Georgia a few years ago is also still a bit raw in some quarters."

"He's not to be trusted, that's for sure," agreed Forsyth. "Ukraine is far from resolved either, by anyone's standards. There will be more to come from Putin in that regard, mark my words."

"Let's just say there is still a mutual distrust between us and the Russians – and I think it will be a long time before it is eradicated." Nicholai stepped from the shower and began to dry himself. Forsyth moved and perched on the edge of the sink. "Telling them my great-great-uncle was Russian didn't exactly help either." Nicholai laughed at the memory of those aghast Russian faces when he told them that part of his family history.

"I didn't know that, Nicholai. You have to tell me more about it when we have time."

Nicholai looked at Forsyth to see if he was joking with that last statement. His deep brown eyes held his gaze and Nicholai realized that his intelligence training was second nature to him. "With respect, sir, when you work on secret military assignments as I do, the MOD, Washington and of course NATO researches your background with a fine tooth comb. You will have read my file and know every detail of my life and my ancestors."

Forsyth gave Nicholai a wry smile and shrugged. "I'm sorry. Of course you are right. Murdered by the Bolsheviks in 1918, wasn't he?"

"Unfortunately for him, he was a count, and cousin of the Tsar!" Nicholai caught a glimpse of himself in the mirror above the sink behind Forsyth. He held his own gaze for a second or two and felt oddly like he was looking into someone else's eyes. It passed and he quickly wrapped the towel around himself, then grabbed another to dry his hair. "Anyway, telling them that little story didn't exactly help matters." He looked at Forsyth and winked at him to lighten the mood. "The Vodka was great though!"

Forsyth laughed and started to leave. "I will see your report in due course. What are your plans for the holidays?"

"I am not due back until the 27th December. So we are spending a few days at the Randolph – Charley and I – for Christmas. Didn't she tell you?"

"Good," replied Forsyth with a smile, "enjoy the break both of you. You know Charley – she always marches to the beat of her own drum. I will see her at some point over Christmas but she never tells me anything. I'm just her uncle!"

"Yes, thank you." Nicholai felt a little uncomfortable at the seemingly casual way Forsyth accepted his niece's indifference. He made a mental note to speak to Charley about it.

Forsyth turned to leave and as he got to the door, he paused and turned back to Nicholai. "I am glad all that unpleasant business didn't harm your career, Nicholai. You should never have been implicated in the first place." Forsyth then seemed rather hesitant but decided to ask anyway. "Do you still see Lovell?"

"No, sir." Nicholai was becoming rather uncomfortable and couldn't believe Forsyth brought this up. "If you don't mind it is something I would rather forget about. It all happened more than a year ago."

"Good job the Russians didn't get wind of it, eh?" He saw Nicholai's discomfort.

"The past is no good to any of us – best left where it is." He smiled reassuringly at Nicholai. "It must be painful when a trusted friend can betray you so easily – and lie to you." Forsyth opened the door to depart. "Merry Christmas!"

As the door clicked shut, Nicholai sat on the edge of the bed and lay back. He was stunned at the questions about Lovell and what happened. Was Forsyth trying to tell him something? Trying to warn him about something perhaps? Did he know something that Nicholai didn't? The situation with Lovell had been all so unpleasant and all so unnecessary, but he was determined not to dwell on it today of all days. His machine made an odd pinging noise and he could see a message. Charley's message, to say she was at the gates to the base and was he ready yet? He rubbed his hair vigorously with the towel, then threw it to one side and started to quickly get dressed.

Charley had arrived at the gates to Brize Norton and had been stopped by the guard on duty. Her attitude made it clear she was less than pleased at not being simply waved through. Her attitude to others was always abrupt or less than polite. She gave the guard her name and after a couple of seconds she saw his face register who she was and then smiled at his apologies. Security was thorough for good reason. He lifted the barrier and she roared into the base without a backward glance or another word to the guard. He watched as she moved off in a cloud of dust. Charley wasn't in the mood for more delays, so hoped that Nicholai was ready and waiting when she arrived at his quarters.

A mile or so away two workmen were in the process of erecting a huge sign, on the specially constructed wooden posts just along the road from the derelict old gatehouse of our home, Willow Manor. The sound of their hammering and drilling, and the men's shouting voices, echoed through the grounds and penetrated the abandoned manor house. Way up in the attic the sound of my dress dragging along the dusty floor swished as I paced the attic corridor. Weak winter sunlight pierced through holes in the roof and illuminated the dancing of the dust particles that swirled in the surrounding air, disturbed by my weary, ethereal presence. The thud, thud sound of the hammering in the distance disturbed me at that, time as I wasn't sure what it was or what it might mean. The screeching metal and the voices seemed to merge into one cacophonous, ugly noise that made my mind whir in confusion and anger. Enraged I transported myself by thought to the entrance hall and waited.

Nicholai smiled at Charley as he made his way from the barrack block to her carriage. He carried his leather weekend case, and at the sight of this, Charley wondered how she would get herself out of a tricky predicament. She pressed the switch that released the lid covering the storage area, and Nicholai threw his case in. He walked to the passenger side of the carriage and as he did so Charley admired his physique and handsome face. His darkness was, she thought, an inheritance from his Russian roots perhaps. In complete contrast his character and accent were very much New York American.

Nicholai's ancestors, or at least some of them on his maternal side, had been among the lucky ones who managed to flee the Russian homeland just before the revolution took hold and slammed its borders shut in 1916. The First World War had been a disaster for Russia and after the Tsar abdicated, they withdrew from the conflict and concentrated on domestic politics, led by Lenin and the Bolsheviks. Nicholai's mother, whose husband was a brother to Count Romanov, managed to escape to England and from there joined a distant cousin on her mother's side, who had fled to New York before the turn of the century, after the infamous and bloody pogroms in Russia. There was Jewish blood on that side of the family, that accounted for the desire to escape the brutal regimes of the Tsars. It was an irony that one of them, her true heritage hidden, would marry into the aristocracy and become connected to the Tsar and his family in later years.

Nicholai's great-great-uncle, Count Nicholai Andreovitch Romanov had been a close friend, cousin and supporter of Tsar Nicholas and his family, and also served as the captain of the royal yacht The Standart! In that role he would became a friend and protector of the young Tsarevitch, sadly afflicted with haemophilia and often seriously ill. This terrible disease is genetic and caused the sufferer to bleed uncontrolled as they lacked the natural clotting elements in the blood. If a bang caused an internal bleed, it could be fatal. In public, it was his job to ensure the world and the press saw the young heir in a positive way. Official photographs were always staged to ensure his image was that of a healthy, happy and confident young boy. The reality was he was weak and rather fragile of health. Nicholai would often carry him, to make sure he was not bumped accidentally, and to prevent him falling against anything, setting off the internal bleeding that so often plagued him and drove the Tsarina to distractions of worry. Nicholai supported the Romanovs. He was loyal until the end and pretended to be a manservant so he could remain with the Imperial family when they were imprisoned at the Tarko Selo, the Summer Palace, then shipped off to various secret holding locations until they eventually arrived at their final place of special purpose, in Ekratinberg.

"Where is your luggage, Charley?" Asked Nicholai as he slipped into the passenger seat beside her. "I noticed there was nothing in the back," he said as he glanced at the empty back seat "What's going on?"

"How was your trip?" she said brightly to try and ease the conversation. "Have you seen my uncle?"

"Nice try, Charley," he said with a suspicious tone in his voice, "something tells me you are up to something." He waited for her reply as she started the carriage and sped off towards the guardhouse.

"I'm not up to anything, Nicholai, it's just work." She glanced across at him to see his reaction. "I have to go back to London tonight," cutting him off before he could protest, she added quickly, "I promise I will be back tomorrow and then I am all yours for the holiday." She waited for his reply but he was silent. The guard lifted the barrier and waved them through onto the Oxford Road and she turned left in the direction of Willow Manor.

"Where are we going now?" is all that he managed to say. He looked from the window as the hedgerow sped past at an alarming speed. "Don't you think you should slow down a little? You'll kill us both at this rate."

Charley slammed on the brakes and he was thrown forward, taken by surprise. "Please don't make an issue of it. It's work, I have to get this new project sorted before we break for Christmas." She looked across at him. "I need to stop off somewhere on the way to Oxford. It won't take long, I promise."

"Whatever, just slow down a little please!" He tightened his grip on his seat belt and then added, "I spoke to your uncle before I left. He didn't know we had plans for Christmas. Do you never communicate with your family?"

"We are calling at that Manor you mentioned, the one you see on your flight path for landing – the one that has always fasci-nated you so much." She gazed across to see him looking at her with a wry smile on his face. "What?" She said wryly.

"Do you never respond to a question with a straight answer?" He looked at her intently. "Remind me why it is I like you so much?" He laughed at her indifference and she eventually broke into a smile. "Fuck you, and your up-tight Britishness!"

"If you play your cards right, you just might get the chance," she replied, laughing out loud at him. He smiled back in spite of his gathering irritation at her stubbornness and inflexible attitude towards their relationship.

It is this behaviour that I recognized immediately as a trait that Charlotte had carried from one life to the next. I understand that now as something far more sinister than once I did as an innocent sister in my past lifetime. She managed to manipulate and cajole to get her own way. I am just astounded that Nicholai cannot see through this and assess her behaviour; or recognise it from the past. Perhaps they are unaware that they have lived before? That I knew them when I was still in possession of my mortal body, long since rotted away, leaving just my bones draped in the remains of my once glorious wedding dress. Are they aware that I knew them and loved them and am still here waiting for them to return, so my spirit can soar to its rest beyond this world I no longer recognize or want to be part of.

Perhaps he has yet to learn the twists and turns of her character, and needs to face this humiliation she heaps on him with such disrespect. In that other life, Nicholai was so loyal and kind. I remember watching helpless, my unseen and un-heard spirit, trapped in this silent world, unable to communicate with the usual senses. Senses we take for granted when you have a heart that beats, blood that flows through your veins. It was the day Lovell read about Nicholai in the Times in 1917, and I followed him to the abandoned and derelict Summer House down by the lake. I knew that Lovell was fond of Nicholai, but I little understood the depth of that feeling and its consequences that terrible day.

The interior of the Summer House was neglected, as it had not been used for many years. I still remember how sunshine streaked through the filthy windows and highlighted the dust and cobwebs. Lovell's footsteps were unsteady, his face incredulous as he stared again at the headlines in The Times. He unlocked the door. His legs were shaking as he walked into the centre of the room. I tried to cry out to him to let him know I was still with him and wanted so much to embrace him and make it better – comfort him in his loss. Then I saw it in his hand, the pistol. I screamed but it was silent. Lovell slowly put the gun to his temple; tears were streaming down his emotionless face. I could see in that moment he felt nothing for this world and was happy to leave it. His eyes were dark and blank.

I wondered if it meant we would be reunited, if he died, that we could be together again. That I would have a companion of my darling Lovell in this spirited hell of an existence. I heard the shattering shot of the pistol as he pulled the trigger. I just watched as, in almost slow motion, his body crumpled, his handsome face contorted into grisly shapes, and blood spurted red and hot across the wall behind him. Fountain-like it sprayed the room as his body slowly collapsed, imploded and hit the floor with a thud. The pupils of his dying eyes frosted over. His newspaper had also fallen onto the floor and the gun in his hand flopped next to it, along with a sepia toned photograph showing us all together and smiling in happier days – the four of us – as we were in 1893. I then saw the headlines "Tsar & Romanov Family Murdered by the Bolsheviks in Ekratinberg" the puddle of blood grew larger and soaked into the paper. Nicholai could be clearly seen standing behind the Tsar and Tsarina in the photograph. He was murdered alongside them. The sound of the breeze carrying a mist across the lake immediately crept into the open summerhouse door, swirling round the decayed and mouldy remains of my dress. It mingled with the steam rising from Lovell's spilt blood.

It took no longer than a few seconds for me to see Lovell's spirit rise from his body. My heart leapt at the thought Lovell would join me and I watched as his soul rose and recognized me. His eyes were pleading and he seemed to mouth the words "I am sorry." "Sorry for what?" I shouted to him. "Don't be sorry, we can be together..." But it was too late, he was carried away – his arms outstretched towards me as if he wanted to take me with him. Slowly his soul dissipated and was gone. "Come back for me," I screamed after him, "please don't leave me here alone.

Lovell, please don't leave me here alone again. You must come back for me." It was no good, he was gone. I didn't understand then why his spirit could not stay with me. It was all part of the reason I am still here. They were all destined to live another life. In time we would all meet again. That was our destiny.

Charley had explained to Nicholai they would be calling at Willow Manor so she could check that the advertising hoarding was in place. Her job as a sales agent for a property development company was her primary interest. Nicholai knew he came way down the line of Charley's priorities. As they began to slow down they could see the workmen putting the final fixings to the huge advertising hoarding near the entrance to the Manor.

Willow Manor Park

'A luxury retirement and residential development of superb 1, 2 and 3 bedroom apartments in this magnificent, former stately home. The park will include a fully equipped leisure centre, ornamental gardens and exclusive lakeside restaurant and bars.
All Enquiries to Rutley & Lord Estates, London 020 1278 4268'

As they got out of the carriage the workmen looked towards them and acknowledged Charley. Nicholai watched as she crossed and chatted to them and then took out her handheld camera machine and began to take some pictures of the advertising hoarding. Nicholai couldn't help but wonder why it was so large and so elaborate. Apart from the descriptive text it had an artist impression of the finished manor house and grounds. This seemed odd to me as it looked nothing like the manor I knew and loved from the past.

He began to walk along the edge of the overgrown boundary and could make out the derelict gatehouse a little further along the road. It was obscured by thick undergrowth and ivy that had crept over and into every crevice of the building. The huge wrought iron gates with our faded family crest were still just visible, along with countless swathes of rusty chains that were interwoven through the gates, secured with old clumps of cast iron, that were once padlocks that locked the gates closed. In the weak winter sunlight he could see little specs of gold glinting here and there – the remains of gold leaf on the finials and decorative areas of the crest. In other areas, streaks of green, oxidized metal disfigured what would once have been highly decorative coats of arms.

I watched them from the gatehouse window. I could clearly see who I thought was Nicholai and Charlotte on the Oxford Road, and the men who had been hammering and screeching hideously for the past few hours. It looked like them, but in other ways I wasn't sure. Their clothes so different, and their hairstyles. The machines the workmen held in their hands made the most terrifying noise and seemed to me to be objects able to inflict terrible injuries. How reassuring it was to know that soon, if it was them, Nicholai and Charlotte would be in my world again. I had never been able to leave the boundaries of the house and grounds until I saw them again – then I could follow them. I remember trying often, a long time since, but it was always impossible to move beyond the gates of the manor or the family graveyard on the opposite boundary, beyond the lake and parkland. I never understood why that was. Like I never understood why I had been cursed to remain here whilst others had died and moved on. It seemed like it was only me that had never been able to follow the natural order of life and death.

Nicholai suddenly became aware of my distorted face, looking at him through one of the gatehouse windows. Shielding his eyes from the winter sun, he peered closely but couldn't see anything. It unnerved him a little but he wasn't sure why.

"What are you looking at?" Charley said, making him jump out of his skin. "Looks a bit creepy doesn't it," she added, pointing to the gatehouse.

"I wish you wouldn't creep up on me like that. I nearly had a heart attack!" He didn't like the sarcastic laugh that blurted out, but let it pass. He was too intrigued by the house to cause another argument.

The workmen had climbed into their large carriage and waved goodbye as they made their way past them on the road back to Oxford. Nicholai looked at the sign again.

"Why is it so enormous? Seems a little over the top for out here."

Charley pointed to the horizon and suddenly Nicholai became aware of the motorway noise in the distance. He noticed she was looking at him in that slightly condescending way of hers.

"I wanted to make sure they could see it from the M40," she said. "At least they will perhaps be intrigued enough to come and take a closer look. At least that is the plan!"

"Remind me," he said with a smile, "why you are such a pain in the ass and why I like you so much?"

Before she could respond he walked off down the road and began to study the gates in more detail. Charley followed him and was obviously relishing the challenge of this project – primarily for the money she would make in the long-term. As she watched Nicholai scrutinizing the area of wall beyond the main gates, she decided she might even get an apartment for herself in this development, as an investment for the future. She could rent it out as a holiday let to rich, gullible Americans or even use it herself as a weekend retreat. It never entered her thoughts she was talking about our home.

I could hear the sound of my skirts dragging along the remains of the gravel drive. I hoped it was only a matter of minutes before Charlotte would step across the threshold of Willow Manor once again. I wanted to make her feel my loneliness and loss and the suffering I had experienced trapped in this place. Make her experience what I had had to endure. Mixed in with these feelings was a sense of expectation and longing to welcome my sister back to our home. There was so much I needed to understand; so much I wanted answers to, so many questions. Why wasn't Lovell also with them? I was so confused at times, if I could have, I would have screeched and screamed in my frustration.

Suddenly I found myself back in the attic corridor. It surprised me because it was not my wish to be here. Usually I move wherever I like by thought alone, but some other force had brought me here to the attic. Ahead of me I could see a large wooden chest surrounded by debris and broken furniture. I walked cautiously towards it and as I did I found myself experiencing something I recognized as severe breathlessness. The lid suddenly moved and I stopped transfixed, as it seemed to tremble like someone was attempting to open it from the inside. The sound of the lid slamming shut, the lid of the trunk, time and time again ricocheted through my mind and reverberated through the manor. The echo of it vibrating the very walls and floors. Suddenly the lid burst open. I looked inside cautiously. Nothing was there apart from the remains of the rotted silk lining. I felt a scream rising, bursting to be free, but no sound emerged. Why does this memory come back and make me see this again and again and again?

Nicholai looked round sharply to see where the scream had come from. Charley looked at him and laughed. "What's the matter?"

"Did you hear that scream – off in the distance somewhere?" He was standing quite still and listening intently, hoping to hear it again perhaps. "I am sure I heard a scream…"

"Probably a bird or farm animal, I didn't hear anything." She started to pull away some ivy and other creepers growing over the old, wooden door in the boundary wall. "Come and give me a hand with this."

They managed to clear the doorway and then discovered it was unlocked. Giving it a good shove with their shoulders, the seized hinges started to creak into life and after a supreme effort the door opened just enough for them both to squeeze through. They walked into a clearing, brushing the undergrowth aside and off their clothes and out of their hair. Willow Manor sat in the distance, looking handsome but sad. The vastness of the façade made it clear how huge the house was. The mist swirled on the lake in the far distance, behind the manor. This added to the slightly eerie atmosphere as they both stood silent and still as they took it all in.

Charley broke the silence. "Well, this is it." After another pause, she added, "Isn't it magnificent?"

"I've seen this place so many times from up in the sky, I never imagined it could look so vast once down here on the ground." He laughed nervously, as if in shock at actually being there. "Who the hell would want to buy it?"

"Plenty of people. It doesn't look much now but it will be very high end, very exclusive and also very expensive to live here once this has been developed."

"Will they demolish it?"

Charley looked at Nicholai aghast. "Hardly! Only an idiot could even consider that!" She realized immediately by the look on his face she had spoken harshly. She softened her voice in the hope it would placate him. "Anyway, its development and resale potential is much greater if you include the history of the place – the Russians and your fellow Americans will love its proximity to hallowed Oxford."

Nicholai was still a little in awe of what he was seeing. "No doubt you'll conveniently forget to mention it's on the flight path of Brize Norton," he said accusingly. "So will they turn it into apartments – but keep the façade of the building?"

"Along with any original interior features that can be incorporated during the development and sub-dividing for the individual apartments. They will probably retain the entrance hall and staircase, and perhaps a couple of formal rooms as communal areas if they can." She looked across at Nicholai and smiled. "Funny to think it once belonged to my family." The shocked look on his face made her burst out laughing.

"You are kidding me, right?

"No, I am being serious. It was purchased by the government just before the Second World War in 1939, when an old family aunt died. They used it for some secret military purpose and it has been empty and derelict ever since about 1946. My great-great-grandfather or something, was the last Baron Forsyth of Littlemore, the title died with him because there was no male heir. "Shall we take a look inside?"

"Does that mean you are titled or something?"

"Technically I am Lady Forsyth, but I never use it." She saw him chuckle. "What's so funny about that?"

"You, a Lady? Give me a break!"

"Thanks. Shall we take a look inside?" She looked at him expectantly. "Well?"

Nicholai was suddenly uncomfortable. He was obviously more than a little apprehensive. "I'm not sure." He pointed to the lake in the far distance. The mist swirling over its surface had intensified. "That is seriously weird, it gives me a very uneasy feeling for some reason."

"Nicholai, it's just the mist – you get it all the time in this part of the world – along with fog, really bad fog. It's because Oxford lies in the basin of the Thames Valley, so it's a naturally occurring phenomenon." He didn't seem convinced, so Charley decided to play with him. "They do say these old places have a soul, you know…"

He swung round alarmed. "Stop right there! If you even go down that road I am off."

Charley laughed at him, surprised that her teasing had elicited such a strong reaction from him.

"I mean it, Charley. Cut it right out." He stormed off towards the house, in spite of himself, and the main entrance loomed over him before he knew it. Charley followed quickly behind him.

I was watching them from an upstairs window. Their argument upset me for some reason. The clothes they wore were strange and nothing like the styles they once favoured. Their hairstyles were also odd, and did nothing to flatter his handsomeness or her strident femininity. Suddenly I was trans-ported back to the night before my wedding. Father had arranged for all the estate servants and their families and children to line the driveway of Willow Manor. After the sun had gone down and it was dark, they all lit candles and created a processional route for me. I made a promenade past them on Father's arm in my engagement gown, Lovell had been banished to his rooms by Father until it was all over, they all cheered, and the children handed me sprigs of mistletoe, to add to my bridal bouquet for the following day's wedding ceremony.

I can see it all again in slow motion, see us as we glided along the drive. Father was so very happy and so proud. The children's faces were beaming and their eyes full of joy for me. There seemed to be nothing but goodwill and smiling faces in the world – especially towards myself and Father and all the family. When we arrived at the entrance, we turned, Father and I, and smiled and waved at all the children and estate servants. Father led me into the entrance hall of the manor, where the house servants were lined up the grand staircase and along the pillared minstrel gallery above, all smiling and cheering. We entered the drawing room and there were Charlotte and Nicholai standing by the fireplace, along with Florence, with the portrait above covered in its silk drapes, concealed until after the wedding.

I then found myself standing at the top of the stairs in the derelict hall. I was watching them again. Nicholai and Charley were standing in the hall at the foot of the once grand staircase, oblivious of me watching their every move, every gesture, and every expression. In spite of the filth, neglect and decay, they could see how magnificent the house had once been. The sadness in the air was almost palpable. The atmosphere of what had been somehow lingered in the hopes that it would be revived. One of the huge double front doors was eaten away with rot, the other barely hanging on its hinges, allowing the elements unfettered access to wreak their havoc. Nicholai pushed away a mound of litter and dead leaves to reveal the extraordinary-tiled mosaic floor. The plasterwork had survived in places and the marble pillars still stood proudly erect and held the minstrel gallery in place. The huge curved and sweeping mahogany staircase was still identifiable beneath layers of brown and green military style paint. Where a huge chandelier had once hung, just the rotted remains of the velvet covered support cable remained, hanging in limbo and gently swaying with the breeze that blew in through missing windows and doors, carrying fallen leaves with it to clog the passages and create that musty smell of damp, decay and neglect.

The enormous, double height, French polished doors that led to the main salon and drawing room were still intact, although covered in the same sickly, green paint. Glimmers of their former glory were revealed here and there, where the paint had bubbled and peeled off because of the dampness and cold. The brass door furniture was missing in places, but what remained was dark and crusty with green oxide. The cobwebs were so numerous they took on the appearance of huge swathes of candyfloss, obscuring perhaps further hidden treasures of the past.

Charley caught Nicholai's eye. "Are you coming up?" She indicated upstairs.

"No, no thanks. You go ahead. I am going to take a look in here." He watched her go off upstairs, gingerly picking her way over debris and rotten stair boards.

Nicholai entered the drawing the room and looked nervously around – his reflection briefly caught in a segment of an old mirror that is attached to the wall, which was much bigger and elaborate at one time, what was left was mottled with damp and age and heavily foxed. I entered close behind him, caught a glimpse of my skeletal form in the mirror fragment, and watched him intently. A huge paint spattered dustsheet that was moth eaten and filthy was hanging above the fireplace. It flapped in the draught. Gingerly he started to walk towards it when there was a huge crash. He jumped and swore, then looked down at his feet and realized he had walked into a clump of discarded, empty, wine bottles and cans. He silently admonished himself for being scared. From the vast window he could see the lake in the distance. He shuddered physically at the sight of it without knowing why.

I watched him as he moved towards the huge windows looking out towards the lake. As he passed the fragment of mirror, I saw his reflection. It made me gasp and I whispered "Nicholai?" His reflection was that of Count Nicholai Romanov, dressed so beautifully in his Russian naval uniform.

"Charley is that you?" He turned sharply towards the doorway. "It's not funny. Are you there?"

I must leave him and find her, I thought. Charley had wandered along the dusty, upper corridors and was drawn towards a particular room. As she entered she sensed a familiarity that confused her but it was no surprise to me. This was one of Charlotte's suite of rooms. They were once beautifully furnished but now, like the rest of the manor, unrecognizable in their decay. Plush drapes, or what remained of them, hung still at the large Georgian windows overlooking what was once the formal rose garden. I was aware that Charley had begun to feel uncomfortable with the dusty atmosphere. She crossed to the window and tried to pull the curtain aside so she could see the view better and open the window. In an instant the remains of the curtains disintegrated into clouds of thick dust. It swirled around her and enveloped her. She began to struggle to breathe, trying desperately to suck in oxygen, but she only made it worse by clogging her lungs with more dust. Collapsing on the floor she began to gasp and try and call out Nicholai's name, but to no avail.

Her bag fell on the floor and the contents spilled out, including her inhaler. She tried to reach it but it was just out of her grasp; her hand clawing and scratching at the bare boards like some deformed spider. All the while she was gasping for air and her lips slowly started to turn blue. Watching her and feeling helpless, I summoned up all the energy I could and cried out, "Nicholai!" and to my surprise I heard the sound of my voice echoing through the empty manor. I then focused my mind; making all the doors, apart from the one to this room, slam shut along the corridor. Their noise resembled the burst of machine gun fire, reverberating through the empty house. Charley was still gasping for air, I know now she was suffering a breathing attack brought on by the dust.

Suddenly, Nicholai burst through the door. He stood looking at Charley whilst she continued to struggle to breathe. His expression was chilling and full of contempt, as if enjoying seeing her suffer like this. I could see that this was Nicholai of 1893. Why was he doing this? Suddenly his face expressed concern and he was again present day Nicholai, and he rushed to her and helped her take puffs of her inhaler.

"Come on, Charley, breathe. Breathe deep breaths, that's it." He held her and helped her to her feet. "Thank God you managed to shout out my name."

"I didn't…"

"Of course you did, you must have, who else could have shouted?"

"I was suffocating," she gasped breathlessly, "for Christ's sake! How the hell could I shout anything?"

"If it wasn't you, who was it?"

"How the fuck should I know. Can we just get out of here, please."

Nicholai supported her and they made their way back down

the staircase. As they passed the remains of a mirror in the hallway, I could see their reflections. It was Nicholai and Charlotte. Now I could only pray they would bring Lovell with them – soon..

It seemed so clear now that I knew the full story, understanding the possibilities of reincarnation, and knew that those three people so dear to me in 1893 had come back in another time to live another life. All the while I was still a trapped soul that seemed destined to roam the house and grounds of my former home for eternity. I understand if you need a moment to make sense of my story. It took the help of Willow Manor to convince me. Their reflections in the Manor's broken mirrors were those of their past incarnation. From this I knew they had returned.

Chapter 3

The Gathering – Christmas Past – December 22nd 1893

Lady Marlborough, my aunt, who usually arrived anywhere with a frenetic flourish of activity, embellished with a large dose of her exuberant eccentricity, was due imminently! Standing a little more than five feet, she was always elegant of appearance, and in spite of her ever-increasing waistline, along with the appearance of a growing widow's hump; she belied her years of more than eight decades. This could also be said for her complexion, in spite of the obvious presence of rouge, shocking in itself for a woman of her station. The years and the death of her husband some decades earlier had taken little toll on her physical appearance and spirit. A cousin to Father, she would always be jolly and amenable of mood. A "joyful irritation" is how Father sometimes referred to her in private. I often marvelled at the fact she had the energy of a woman half her age and the common sense of one twice her age and experience. She had, I see now, always been a very wise and knowing soul. Perhaps I should have appreciated her more in my lifetime and sought her wise council. Instead, as with all youth, I only saw her age and thus inevitable irritability.

Her arrival for my wedding was fast approaching, the reason why there was a rush of last minute activity by the servants to complete preparations, in itself a testament to the greatness of her reputation and colossal personality. On that fateful day of 22nd December 1893, my father was dressing in readiness for greeting the guests arriving for the wedding, at least those who would be staying as houseguests, prior to the Christmas Eve ceremony – and indeed for the Christmas festivities that would naturally follow. In spite of some years passing since my mother's death it had been decided to keep the wedding as a quiet, family occasion. Father hated nothing more than a fuss or crowds. As a result we were few, not counting the estate and house servants. Andrews, the family butler, along with Florence and the house staff were busily trying to finish the decorations in the Grand staircase and entrance hall.

Andrews was a contemporary of Florence. I was never completely sure of his actual age but he was, I estimated, less than sixty years but more than fifty. He had been a very handsome man in his youth, standing imposingly at nearly six-feet tall. As a result he towered over most of the servants and thus received their unquestioning respect. The handsomeness of his roman features had matured into a pleasing face with hardly any trace of wrinkles, with almost pure white hair, beautifully groomed and always impeccable in his appearance. His crowning glory was his magnificent nose, that gave him an imperiousness unmatched in the household. He also had beautiful hands, a rare thing for a man, fingers long and masculine, with highly manicured nails that fascinated me. His skills as a butler had served the family since the time my mother was alive. As with most staff at the Manor, be they domestic or estate, if they fitted in to the demands of the family, they likely stayed forever.

As a result of this, Andrews was of course close in his working relationship with Florence. Their respective sitting rooms and offices were side by side in the labyrinth that was the servant's quarters and kitchens that lay behind and beyond the green baize door, down a twisting staircase, into the lower ground floor of the Manor. This was an area that the family seldom visited unless either invited by Florence or Andrews, or some crisis or drama demanded them to do so in an emergency. On the odd occasion I ever ventured down into that unknown industrious world, it always struck me how scrubbed and clean it was, the odd smell of disinfectant, where footsteps and other sounds echoed in the corridors compared to upstairs. The further one ventured towards the kitchens, I remember twitching my nose because of the strange smell of carbolic soap and boiling cabbage. Once, as I passed, I saw Andrews in the vault room cleaning the silverware. He stood rubbing vigorously a table salver, his white shirtsleeves covered with green slipovers to prevent them from getting dirty. The family silver was his pride and joy and he personally polished every item himself. His labour was an example of the pride the servants took in their work for Father. The smell of the acrid polish mingled with the other aforementioned smells to create an odour quite unique to that part of the Manor.

Between them Florence and Andrews managed the house and all the domestic servants therein. The few days leading up to Christmas had been fraught with added responsibilities in terms of ordering supplies and preparing guest suites because of the wedding. Sweeping chimneys and black-leading bedroom fireplaces before lighting them to help air the rooms was a mammoth operation in itself – especially as many of these rooms had not been used for some years, mostly shrouded in dust sheets that had themselves become dust laden! The Christmas decorations in the formal living rooms were also far from complete and time was running out. One of the footmen, I remember, burst through the green baize door from the servant's hall, carrying a box of decorations, only to nearly collide with Andrews, who was far from amused.

"For heavens sake, Ashworth, be careful what you are doing," barked Andrews in exasperation at this lack of decorum. He shook his head as a sign meant to punctuate his disapproval and Ashworth slowed down as a result. "Take those straight through to the dining room, Ashworth." He gestured with a wave of his arm to move along. Andrews then caught sight of the housemaid, Millie, perched atop a pair of stepladders attempting to attach a garland across the doorway.

"Millie! What on earth?" Millie turned instinctively in panic at being addressed so directly. She looked down at Andrews, in doing so began to lose her balance and wobble precariously, all the while desperately trying to retain her composure and hide her fear.

"I'm sorry, sir." With the panic and fear of falling all in the tone of her voice, that lurched to a shrill on the last syllable. "Frightened me half to death," she muttered under her breath, then added, "can I help you, sir?" She just about managed to regain her balance atop the stepladder in time to hear his retort.

"How many times must I tell you," he boomed impatiently, "only the mistletoe garlands are to be draped across the doorways." He looked at her nonplussed expression and sighed with despair at her seeming stupidity. "Well? Have you nothing to say, Millie? Do you understand my instructions or not, girl?"

During this exchange, Millie could see Molly the scullery maid out of the corner of her eye and also Stevens the younger footman. He had entered and stood at the foot of the ladder to help steady it for her. From this vantage point he looked up at her with a knowing look in his eye; trying to warn her to avoid answering back Andrews at all costs. Molly had stopped her scrubbing of the mosaic-tiled floor and watched open mouthed as Millie tried very hard to keep a straight face. For some reason she found herself on the verge of laughing at the ridiculousness of the situation she was in. A lower servant in conversation with Andrews – it should never have happened. The likes of the butler barely recognized the existence of a mere housemaid like herself, she thought. Except perhaps when a fire grate needed cleaning out or a bucket of coal needed hauling up five flights of cold, back stairs. She became highly visible then. She found all these thoughts going through her mind and as a result time seemed to freeze. After a moment, she found herself back in the present, with Andrews staring up at her, obviously waiting for her reply to some unheard question. She decided that if she opened her mouth to speak she would likely release the inexplicable laughter trapped at the back of her throat.

"Impertinent girl," he fumed and glared at her, "and don't mutter under your breath when I speak to you or else you may find yourself in the scullery or looking for an alternative position."

"I am sorry, Mr Andrews, sir." She managed at last without the laughter following – much to her relief. "I will make sure only the mistletoe garlands are used here, sir."

"Well get on with it, girl! We haven't got all day." He looked around at the others. "Stevens, help Millie." He noticed Molly then, staring and frozen to stillness. "Come along there, get on with it!" She immediately started scrubbing where she had left off before the altercation. He watched as Stevens handed Millie the correct mistletoe garland for the doorway. "We have yet to organize the decorations in the chapel." Suddenly remembering something important, he addressed Stevens. "Have you removed the dust sheets from the ballroom chandeliers yet, Stevens?"

"Yes, Mr Andrews," he replied politely, with a wink at Millie. "They have all been cleaned and new candles have replaced the used ones."

"Splendid! Let's get on now." He crossed to Molly and started to point out defects in the floor she was cleaning. She responded by scrubbing with more vigour than before. She seemed more terrified that he was actually speaking to her at all than by what he was saying.

Millie had climbed down the ladders, so Stevens could reposition them for her to attach the centre part of the garland. She looked to make sure Andrews was out of ear shot and then muttered to Stevens, "Why is nothing I ever do 'splendid'," she sighed in resignation. "I don't suppose he cares much for me now."

"He just likes things to be correct in every way," he whispered, all the while smiling at her. He watched as Millie started blushing. "He has a lot on his mind and well..."

Millie found herself getting more and more embarrassed because this was the first time she had actually spoken properly to Stevens, and more to the point, the first time she had noticed how striking he was and how lovely his eyes were. As a result she felt the hotness of her cheeks and was horrified to find herself blushing – knowing he would see and realize what was going through her mind.

"Maybe someone has taken his fancy," Stevens said to Millie with a knowing wink, "they say he has been flirting with Florence."

"Never! That man would frighten any woman to a distance of a hundred miles," she blurted out incredulous at the thought, "and further on a clear day, too!"

Stevens laughed with Millie and then they were brought to silence by the sound of voices on the gallery above. Lord Lovell and Count Romanov were making their way downstairs to the drawing room. The servants busied themselves with their tasks and neither spoke, nor acknowledged the guests personally. Millie, from the corner of her eye, was immediately struck at how handsome Count Romanov looked, as he seemed to gallop down the curving staircase, with Lord Lovell close behind him. His physical power and personal charisma overshadowed that of Lord Lovell's. His dominance was always apparent.

My father, Baron Forsyth was standing with his back to the fire in the main drawing room, awaiting the arrival of our house-guests. His stature had waned over recent years and as a result his temperament seemed somewhat irascible to those unfamiliar with his manner. His height was no more than five feet six and his once fair hair had turned to grey, although the uneven tones made it look dull. His features were by this time worn down by the disappointments and grief life had placed on his shoulders. However, I am pleased to say, his face could still light up when he chose to smile and on occasion the twinkle, or at least remnants of it, flashed across his weary, watery blue eyes. His habit of twiddling his lower waistcoat button gave an indication of his impatience or annoyance over some misdemeanour or remark in whatever company he was keeping. I always knew to distract him or an unwary guest at such times, to save them from the cutting remark he would always let escape in spite of his usual good manners.

He turned and lifted the silk cloth covering the portrait of me he had commissioned as a wedding gift and was suitably pleased with what he saw. In spite of the subject being myself, it reminded him of my late mother. That, I guessed pleased him more, and was also, I suspected, the truth behind his desire to commission the painting. I felt no insult or hurt at this obvious fact, indeed I was flattered that my father would complement me so. A loud knocking at the door signalled that guests were about to enter. My father turned and smiled as Andrews opened the door and announced Count Romanov and Lord Lovell.

"Lovell, my dear boy." He grasped Lovell's hand and never took his eyes off Nicholai.

"Thank you, sir, it is good to see you again," replied Lovell warmly. "May I introduce you to Count Nicholai Romanov."

"Count Romanov, you are also welcome." Grasping his hand for a formal handshake, "I am delighted to welcome you to my home and also to my daughter's wedding to Lovell."

Andrews withdrew from the drawing room and closed the doors with quiet efficiency.

"Thank you, sir." Nicholai seemed to appraise Father and then decide he liked him. "Please call me Nicholai, or Nicky if you prefer. The latter is easier for the English tongue, I believe?"

"Perhaps so, I never considered it before but you could be right. However," he said, smiling warmly, " I think I prefer Nicholai and it respects your heritage." He laughed and then added, "Lovell has told me so much about you."

Nicholai looked at Lovell with surprise at this revelation. He was also aware that the baron was impressed with his command of spoken English – with hardly any trace of his native Russian accent. "You seem surprised at my English, sir? The result of my education at the Tsar's court in St Petersburg, then at Eton and Oxford, of course."

"We first met at Eton," interjected Lovell, "at the age of six but didn't become friends until years later, when thrust together when we went up to Oxford."

"We spent so much time together," said Nicholai, "we became very close friends, until we left Oxford to join our respective Navy careers." He looked warmly at Lovell. "I have missed our friendship but feel glad to be here today in your beautiful home, sir."

My father was so impressed with Nicholai, and delighted that someone so near the Tsar's imperial family was enjoying the hospitality of Willow Manor. But he would not express this for fear of seeming to want to exploit such a connection in some way. Like most Englishmen of his aristocratic class, he said little to suggest he was impressed or delighted to be favoured by those with royal connections. Such overt behaviour would strike many as vulgar and inappropriate.

Lovell's attention was drawn to my still covered portrait above the fireplace. "Are you pleased with it, sir? I can't wait to see it." He attempted to take a sly look behind the silk cover. But Father secured it from his view. Poor Lovell, so near and yet so far and he detested secrets and having to wait for anything. Only now, after more than a century of waiting, could I empathize with him fully.

"Damn fine, Lovell, just like her mother," Father exclaimed with pride, "which means you are a damn lucky fellow!"

"I am looking forward to meeting your daughters," Nicholai said warmly. "Lovell has told me all about them; especially Lady Ellen of course..."

Lovell looked at Nicholai nervously, fearing he might be

about to voice the concerns he had about our marriage. Instead Nicholai smiled warmly at Father and gave Lovell a reassuring wink that instantly put him at ease again.

I wish I had known all this at the time it was happening but alas I didn't. I had no idea that Nicholai was against the marriage; I had no idea that Lovell was guarding secrets that could have destroyed everything at the time. I was ignorant of so many facts and only managed to understand the full story I can now relay to you, once my soul had been released from its burden of haunting the manor. Part of my redemption is to share it here with you; it allows me to be free of all things mortal. Suffice to say that I am learning much now I have the whole picture of events before me. We must continue, my time is not endless for this task and there is much yet I have to place before you.

"Please gentlemen, be seated and make yourselves comfortable," said Father as he crossed and pulled the servants' bell cord a couple of times, to summon Andrews. He re-joined them by the fireplace. "I am so glad you agreed to be Lovell's best man, especially as he has no family of his own to speak of."

"The pleasure," replied Nicholai, "is all mine, sir."

"I do have a great-aunt, twice removed, whom I have yet to meet!" blurted out Lovell, as if embarrassed by his lack of relatives. There was a brief silence, then Lovell laughed good-humouredly at his own foolishness and they join in. This lightened the moment somewhat and the awkwardness of first meetings at last began to recede apace.

"How are you finding your new position at the Admiralty, Lovell?" asked Father as he warmed his hands at the fire, then turning still rubbing them vigorously to retain the warmth.

"Challenging, sir. I must admit that bb-being on dry land permanently also has its strains, but it will be perfect once Ellen and I are married. B-being at sea for months and years at a time is not conducive for a good marriage."

A knock at the door brought the discussion to a halt. Andrews entered the room. Father looked at Nicholai and Lovell. "Tea, gentlemen?" They nodded their acceptance and Father turned to Andrews. "Some tea for our guests please, Andrews."

"Indian, Russian or China, sir?" he asked and looked expectantly at Nicholai and Lovell.

"Indian, I think," said Father, then looked at them for their acceptance of his choice. "But if you prefer Russian, Nicholai?"

"No, sir, Indian will be most enjoyable. Thank you."

"There we have it, Andrews, Indian for now please."

"Very good, sir." Andrews backed out and closed the door. Father then added a couple of large logs to the fire and poked it into life. They watched as the flames licked the logs frantically, as the embers grew brighter beneath them.

"Does Ellen know we have arrived," asked Lovell to break the silence, "I haven't seen her or Charlotte."

"Of course they know!" replied Father aghast. "With women in the house, you can't hide anything from them. They know every move and every coming and going – unless they pretend ignorance. The latter would only be to suit themselves or some alternative plan, motive or contrivance. You have much to learn about women, Lovell!"

Lovell was of course impatient to see me and his enthusiasm was such that he seemed uncomfortable in his skin. My father's teasing, and Nicholai's obvious disapproval, I put down to his being irritated with what he perceived to be rather adolescent behaviour. Nicholai and my father responded to each other with an instant rapport and seemed to have known each other longer than the few hours since Nicholai's arrival at Willow Manor. It added a rather strange dimension to the relationship between the three men because my father and Lovell had had a rather stilted relationship, in spite of both trying their hardest to please the other.

"Will Ellen be joining us for ttt-tea, Baron?" asked a rather nervous Lovell, his latent stammer appearing as testament to his increasing anxiety. "Miss Charlotte ttt-too?"

"Plenty of time yet," replied my embarrassed father. He would not acknowledge the appearance of the stammer because Victorian fathers seldom acknowledged what they saw as something less than perfect. "Patience is a virtue, boy." He looked at Nicholai for support. "Wouldn't you agree?"

"A virtue I have never possessed myself, Baron," said Nicholai with obvious concern for Lovell. "And you, sir?"

"With age, I regret to say, it becomes a rather constant companion!" replied Father.

My father's rather wistful reply came across as more wit laden than actually intended. This broke the moment and the three of them laughed. It allowed them to turn a corner and Lovell visibly relaxed – as did they all.

"I have explained to N–Nicholai, that the wedding is to be a fairly quiet occasion," said Lovell to open a new topic of conversation. "Just close family for the service Christmas Eve afternoon, and then some local family friends and house staff for the evening celebration."

"Yes." My father smiled, his gaze turning to Nicholai. "Out of respect to my late wife – I find crowds of people intolerable since her death."

"I was saddened to hear of your loss, sir," replied Nicholai. "Time is not always a great healer. Sometimes one's loss can be too great."

An uneasy silence enveloped them and Lovell could see the wateriness swirling in my father's eyes. Nicholai silently reproached himself for being too direct and igniting an emotional response in my father whilst referring to my late mother. A gentle knocking at the door broke the moment and my father gathered himself and shouted for the knocker, to enter.

Andrews entered, followed by Millie, the housemaid, laden with a huge tea tray that seemed twice her width and impossibly heavy, going by the concentrated, strained expression on her face.

She managed the few short strides to the side table Andrews indicated to, thankfully able to deliver her burden safely and without incident. The relief on her face was visible and almost audible if the long, almost whispered sigh was any indication. Andrews looked at her with a withering disapproval at this unwelcome but audible exhalation of breath; another breach of protocol to be addressed once back in the servants hall. For Millie the concern was more focused on the fine bone china tea service, heavy silver tray and teapot, along with an equally heavy hot water pot and accompanying spoons, milk and sugar receptacles. All, as far as she was concerned, a nasty accident waiting to happen with one missed footing or one second's lapse of concentration. Her sigh, if inappropriate, worthy reward for the relief she felt at that moment. She smiled dutifully at Andrews and bobbed a curtsy to Father and his guests before preparing the tea things to serve. Andrews then attempted to catch the attention of my father.

"Apologies for interrupting, sir," he said sincerely but aware that Father was not of a mind to engage with him, "I need to discuss…"

"What is it man?" Father said rather too abruptly and although irritated at being interrupted regretted the harshness of his tone. He smiled at Lovell and Nicholai and then at Andrews by way of demonstrating an apology of sorts, instead of saying it, which protocol would have made difficult. "You can see that I am busy with our guests, Andrews, can't it wait?"

"There is a problem with the festive tree for the great hall," offered Andrews in the usual calm, professional manner he always employed when Father was of ill humour or vexed, adding, "the estate manager needs your guidance, sir."

"Good God, man!" fired back Father, tempering the comment with a laugh, for the sake of his guests, to demonstrate his disbelief that such a question should be asked of him at such a time. "I have guests to attend to – he'll just have to wait."

Charlotte's entrance at that moment stole the attention away from them. She smiled knowingly at Andrews in such a way that indicated a silent form of communication, well developed between them over many years, that he immediately understood as a request to end the discussion and his quick withdrawal would be appreciated. Andrews began to leave, whilst Nicholai watched with increasing fascination and respect the command Charlotte had over the running of the house and the servants.

"Father will attend to it presently, Andrews." She locked eyes with him, leaving him in no doubt as to who was in charge at this moment. She then held up a black bow. "I found this with a pile of others. No mourning bows on the tree this year. Mother would not have wanted black bows of remembrance at Ellen's wedding, just happy memories of her life with us as a family." Before he had time to respond, she handed him the bow, then turned her attention to Millie, who had been silently setting out the tea things. "I will see to the tea, Millie. You may go." This last command was also directed at Andrews. As he exited she added as an afterthought, "If I am not mistaken, my aunt's carriage is about to arrive, so she will need your assistance with her luggage."

The drawing room doors closing with a soft swish brought their attention back to Charlotte. All eyes were on her. She always savoured such moments. I had witnessed it often, and because it was so daring a thing for any woman to do, it filled me with a sense of awe at her strength of character, and dread at the possible consequences for such overt behaviour in company; especially of men. Father seemed to have resigned himself to the fact that it was a trait in her character, although regarded as a flaw in society, he would have to tolerate it, as he knew it was pointless to try and reprimand or change her. Charlotte's spirit was irrepressible, even for a Victorian father like ours. After a pause she crossed the room towards Father, handing him a cup of tea.

"Now, don't forget what the good doctor said." She kissed him on the cheek and Father blushed slightly at this obvious display of affection. "You mustn't become too excited!"

"Nonsense," replied Father tersely. "The man can be an imbecile at times."

Nicholai watched as she immediately commanded the room and made sure they were all served with tea and the prerequisite polite chatter afforded guests at such an occasion. In his mind he knew that it was all an act. Like an actress in a play, taking control of the part she had been required to bring to life. He could see the emptiness behind each line, each sentiment, no matter how seemingly sincere and exquisite was the delivery of every word. Nicholai knew that Charlotte operated on another level of human consciousness to others – especially her father and Lovell, who were completely engaged by her and oblivious to her clever tactics. He watched as they smiled and laughed at the attention and thought them fools indeed. This woman, he thought, would thrive in the viciousness of the St Petersburg Court with its gossip, treachery and intrigue. Charlotte would, he decided, survive well, even in piranha-infested waters. She caught his eye. In that instant, less than the time it takes for a heart to beat, she knew he saw through her facade. They had a shared past, albeit a fleeting moment in the scheme of life, but they had encountered one another before. Had it not been for that, Nicholai would have perhaps taken longer to analyse my sister and come to know what she so cleverly concealed – even from me at that time.

"Count Romanov," said Father more grandly than was necessary, "this is my daughter Charlotte. She has the responsibility for running the house and servants since her mother's death." He smiled and then added with no sense of the hurt it could inflict, "No harm in being a spinster, is there my dear, especially now your younger sister is to be married." There was a strained silence before he added with a smile, "We all have our place in this life – it is the way of things. Charlotte's place is here, with me, at Willow Manor." I still shudder at the thought of such cruelty delivered with no thought as to the hurt it would inflict on my sister. Charlotte had learned to hide her feelings due to such comments many years before. Charlotte handed Lovell tea and he kissed her hand gallantly.

"Hello, my dear, you look well as ever." She smiled at him warmly and then turned her attention to Nicholai.

"Why, Count Romanov, I do believe we have already had the pleasure?" She smiled at him brightly and found herself amused at the stunned silence at this revelation.

"Indeed, Charlotte, I remember the occasion quite clearly – in fact I recognized you instantly." He looked at Charlotte with an amused expression that wasn't quite a smile but could be miscon-strued as a scowl. Their eyes locked for an instant and a flash of memory replayed in Nicholai's mind.

He had met Charlotte at the Randolph Hotel in Oxford a year or so previous. She had flirted with him throughout the dinner party and again in the ballroom, later the same evening. They never exchanged much conversation as she was escorted by Lady Battenberg's daughter, an unattractive and rather waspish creature, he recalled, with few charms to her credit. Charlotte had caught his attention because, unlike most English aristocratic women, she seemed to send somewhat engaging signals of attraction and appeared unafraid to toy with him. It amused him and he decided to see how far she was willing to go in this bold game of hers. She went far enough to allow him to slip into her room in the early hours and was unabashed in her desire to bed him as quickly as possible. The experience chilled him. As Nicholai looked at her in the assembled drawing room of Willow Manor, it was impossible to imagine Charlotte was the same woman. Indeed she gave no hint of such immoral behaviour. The rest of us were, of course, oblivious to this shocking event at the time – as unthinkable for me now as it would have been for

Father and I that other lifetime ago.

"You two have met before?" said my father in obvious amazement. Lovell also seemed confused that such an event had occurred and he was unaware of it. "It seems impossible to believe an acquaintance has been formed – perhaps fate, dear boy," added my father to Lovell.

"I escorted Grand Duchess Maria, a cousin, to a dinner held by Lady Battenburg at the Randolph in Oxford," Nicholai informed them with a flourish to hide his sudden embarrassment. "Charlotte was among the guests. We chatted, but I had no idea she was related to Lovell's fiancé at that time. I recognized her only when I arrived here today."

"Of course," said Father, "I remember the occasion now. Why didn't you say you had met Count Romanov, Charlotte?"

"I hardly spoke to him at the time Father," replied Charlotte, "and to be frank I didn't realize it was the same Nicholai that was such a close friend of Lovell's or otherwise I would have done." The look they exchanged belied the dislike they held for each other.

Suddenly an almighty noise was heard out in the hallway that brought the current topic of discussion to an end – much to the relief of Nicholai and Charlotte. My aunt's voice could be heard in the distance issuing instructions for luggage and its care in transit to her suite of rooms. The drawing room doors burst open and a rather flustered Andrews entered. He began to announce her rather breathlessly.

"Lady Marl…"

"Well hurry up my good man," interjected my aunt's voice from the hallway. "I have no desire to wait out here all afternoon!"

"Lady Marlborough," he said again firmly, his usual decorum having returned, "has arrived, sir."

My aunt swept into the room with hat in hand and brandishing a pair of pinz-nez. She always gave the impression of being en route to something more important than that she was currently engaged in. Her sheer energy always shocked us, for she seemed to be accelerated by some invisible force that put the rest of us to shame.

"Cousin," she said, "how are you? I am quite well before you ask." Discarding her hat, she spotted the tea tray and then, before Father could answer her, exclaimed with delight, "Tea! I am in dire need of refreshment after that loathsome carriage journey from Witney."

"Delighted to see you, Constance. You are well as ever I see..."

"Never felt better! Although these long carriage rides are anathema to my considerably aged constitution. No matter!"

She dutifully kissed Father, Lovell and Charlotte but all the while her beady eye was fixed on poor defenceless Nicholai – who watched transfixed as this aged woman – who for some reason lifted his spirits, and fascinated him in equal measure, charged forth.

"However," she continued, discarding her cup and saucer to a side table, without as much as a sip of her tea, "there is nothing like a wedding to aid the powers of rejuvenation." She suddenly stopped short and looked intently at Charlotte for a few seconds. Everyone else waited expectantly (it felt as if she sucked all the air from the room – leaving none for the rest of them to use in speech). "Charlotte," she said eventually, "your complexion is terrible! Take my advice, a teaspoon of Laudenum every other morning works absolute wonders." She then fixed her gaze on Nicholai and addressed him directly. "I have been taking it for years and the effects are remarkable!" She winked at him and he couldn't help but smile, as did the rest, at the gorgeous eccentricity of my aunt.

"You have already met Lord Lovell," interjected my father as quickly as he could between her breathing, lest he lose the opportunity to get a word in. Lovell dutifully and formally kissed her hand. Father then indicated to her main point of interest in the room at that moment. "And this is Count Nicholai Romanov, cousin of the Tsar and Lovell's Best Man at the wedding."

"My word," she announced with little decorum, "you are handsome enough to make me feel quite young again." She continued to survey him admiringly, much to Father's consternation and Charlotte and Lovell's amusement. "May I call you Nicholai? I hate formality with titles, so dreary, don't you think?

"A pleasure to make your acquaintance, Lady Marlborough."

"The pleasure is all mine." She then added with contrived wistfulness, "Age can sometimes be a terrible burden, Count."

"Please, call me Nicholai."

"I have heard it said," she added with a smile, "that Russians can be extremely passionate towards life. Is that true, Nicholai?

"Constance! Please," interjected my father, "you are embarrassing our guest."

"Don't be so stuffy, cousin!" shot back my aunt. "And you nearly twenty years younger than me. I only asked as an observation because I am interested. The moment we lose interest in youth, life and other cultures we are doomed. Isn't that so, Nicholai?" She smiled at him and her humour shone through and became infectious. This of course dissipated any tension that had built up and a new corner was turned in the conversation. "Now," she said looking about her, "where did I put that tea." She located it and duly sipped it from her cup as if nothing amiss had ever been said. "Are you looking forward to married life, Lovell?"

"Very much, ma'am."

"Do you know, I still remember mine vividly."

"It is heartening," said Father, "to see him so keen on his last day of bachelorhood – absolute terror is all I remember."

"Something I have yet to experience," said Nicholai with an air of sadness to his voice, immediately picked up by Lady Marlborough, who smiled and said nothing.

"Pay no attention to them, Lovell," said Charlotte entering the conversation with determination. "I consider it a most charming attribute to marry for love as opposed to gaining wealth and connections."

"Thank you, Charlotte," replied Lovell. "I appreciate your kk-kind words and look forward to you as my sister-in-law.

Lady Marlborough turned her attention, and everyone else's, once more to Nicholai. "I take it you are not yet married?"

Nicholai caught sight of himself in the mirror on the far side of the room. For an instant he seemed to see his own image reflected back at him but in strange clothes. The room in the mirror was dark and derelict and seemed full of decay – bearing little resemblance to the reality. As if all the people and furniture around him were not in that other room beyond the mirror. Suddenly the mirror's reflection was normal again and he found he had broken out into a cold sweat. Confused by what he had seen, he then realized Lady Marlborough was waiting for his reply.

"No, something I have yet to experience." He took a handkerchief from his pocket and wiped the sweat from his brow, "My career is my marriage."

"That is unfortunate, Nicholai," said my aunt with real sadness. "Are you quite well?"

"Yes, ma'am, quite well. Just a little too hot standing so close to the log fire."

"An admirable if not lonely substitute, wouldn't you say Nicholai? A career could never replace the warmth of family and children, could it?"

"Nicholai," interjected Lovell to help his friend, "has been asked by his cc-cousin, Tsar Nicholas, to take cc-command of the Imperial Yacht – the Standart!

"A great honour for you," said Father, "will you take up the post in the New Year, Nicholai?"

"Indeed I will, sir. The Standart is undergoing a refit and will be ready for trials in the early spring – in time for the Tsar and his family to attend Cowes week."

"Glorious! I had no idea you were so intimate with the Tsar," gushed Lady Marlborough. "You must tell me all about the St Petersburg Court – I hear that it is remarkable. Of course you are aware that your Tsarina, Alexandria Federova, is a relative of our own dear Queen Victoria and Princess of Wales? And also the Tsar is a cousin of our Royal Family also?"

Andrews knocking and entering the drawing room halted the conversation much to my aunt's annoyance and everyone else's relief. Andrews addressed Father conspiratorially.

"Sir, your presence is required..."

"If you will all excuse me," said Father, not a little exasperated, "I must attend to the Christmas tree. I shall look forward to seeing you all at dinner tonight." He exited muttering about the incompetence of the estate servants and the staff generally.

My aunt continued to entrance Nicholai with her tales of society and gossip. As a result they formed an instant bond of friendship that in some ways allowed each to relax and enjoy what was to come with the wedding and then Christmas. For my part I was excited to see Lovell and also to meet Nicholai. My naivety embarrasses me now, but then I was full of excitement and love, as with any young bride to be. Florence, as always, watched over us with a protective eye. Our guests, along with the rest of us, retired to our respective suites and rooms in order to rest, bathe and prepare for dinner later that evening. The servants were busy fulfilling their roles in the preparations. There seemed nothing amiss, and that nothing could go wrong in the hours and days to come. Or so I thought. The time flew and before we all knew it December 24th was tomorrow.

Chapter 4

The Dinner Party – December 23rd 1893

It pains me now to realize that as I rested, before we convened for the dinner party at eight that December evening, my sister Charlotte had been planning and conspiring to cause trouble, but I never imagined that her actions would be those of such a dark, spiteful and embittered mind.

High in the attic corridors of Willow Manor, where usually only the servants would venture in search of stored furniture, the estate archives or other such items, were a warren of passages and service areas and stairs. It was also where our seasonal wardrobes were placed to make more room in our respective dressing rooms. Father also stored a lot of Mother's personal items and furniture there. At times, when he could be found nowhere else on the estate, Florence or Andrews would invariably look there as a last resort and find him sitting among Mother's belongings and silently weeping for his lost love.

It was in that area of dusty unused attics that a stable groom, under the instructions of Charlotte, had been slowly moving a large piece of furniture to a more accessible corridor, one that could be easily entered up a few service stairs, off the main bedroom corridor in the centre wing of the manor. His task had been arduous as it had required him to move this large item a considerable distance from a far, and rarely used, wing of the manor, and necessitated lifting the item down several short attic and service staircases – unseen or heard by any of the servants or family; aside from Charlotte of course, who had instigated the whole thing. If only I had known. If only either Father, Florence or Andrews had discovered what was going on and had been able to halt this terrible plan before its execution. But alas we were drifting along ignorant of it all. As is usual, it is easy to look back and see what could have been done differently

Father had arranged for a small dinner party to take place on the evening prior to my wedding and wanted it as a small family affair. He had arranged it thus so he would have a chance to get to know our new guest intimately and also as a way of putting Nicholai at ease as he was in unfamiliar company and surroundings. It was a thoughtful thing to do and I didn't mind in the least. If I am honest I wasn't very fond of large gatherings or parties, they always left me shy and at a loss if social chatter and niceties were required.

Whilst we were resting and our guests were settling in to their rooms, the servants were making sure all the necessary preparations were underway and that the decorations were all hung and the tree in the main hall decorated to perfection. Andrews had taken charge in the dining room and was making sure the table was laid with precision and care and that only the best silver, china and linens were used for that special evening. New candles had been trimmed and placed in the wall sconces and in the four, twelve arm candelabra adorning, at precise intervals, the long mahogany formal dining table. The ceiling chandeliers would not be lit, to allow for a more intimate, cosy feeling; but nevertheless they were cleaned and new candles positioned with the erectness and perfection of soldiers in a military parade. Details mattered to Andrews and it always showed on these important family occasions.

The walls of the dining room were adorned with ancestors of both sexes in either their fine silks or formal court dress. They stared down with a look of longing in their eyes that always made me laugh to myself. It was as if they could see and smell the delicious meals and were longing to experience the taste and flavours for themselves once again! One paternal aunt was the exception, she looked on with a withering and soured look as if she found it all rather distasteful to behold and certainly didn't approve. The candlelight always gave these portraits an animated feeling and it was disconcerting to imagine seeing fleeting expressions pass across their brushed, lifeless faces. It was one reason why Father had refused to have all the formal rooms wired with the new electric lights. He hated the glare and the coldness of the light they gave off and restricted its use to some of the staff areas and the landings upstairs. He loved the warmth and atmosphere created by candlelight, as did I.

During that brief spell where the family and guests were busy at their toilet, and the servants equally so below stairs in the kitchens, Charlotte and Nicholai had met in the latter's private sitting room of his suite. The history of their past meetings were as yet unknown to the rest of us. Now I see beyond my naivety at the time, realizing that their acquaintance, if that is what you could call it, was far beyond what I was capable of thinking or understanding at the time. Nicholai was wary of Charlotte, for good reason.

"I cannot understand why you would wish to speak with me about anything," exclaimed Nicholai as he answered the door to her furtive knocking. "Anything you have to say is of no interest to me anymore."

Charlotte was struck by the coldness of his words and felt herself take a sharp intake of breath. It seemed to cut her throat inside and leave her unable to form any words. She collected herself as quickly as she could, all the while searching his eyes for any sign of warmth or caring. Neither was in evidence. "We need to agree an understanding. It is the least we can do for Ellen and Lovell and also my father. Remember you are his guest and owe him that respect at least."

Nicholai suppressed a cynical laugh as he made sense of her words. "My respect for your father," he said finally, "and your sister and my friend knows no bounds. The opposite indeed of the contempt for which I hold you in, Charlotte."

He looked into her eyes with such intensity she felt rather faint and had to hurriedly compose herself and not allow him to intimidate her.

"You have come here to speak to me for your own sake, not theirs. Do you think me that foolish to be unable to see right through your scheming and despicable self-preservation?" He held his eyes locked to hers for what seemed an eternity.

"What passed between us will remain between us," she said defiantly. "There is no need for anyone else to know, is there?" She searched his face for some sign that he would agree. She was angered at the coldness, the aloofness that coated him like he was made of wax. Nothing, no expression flickered through the façade to indicate any glimmer of friendliness. "If my father knew what had passed between us he would have you driven off the estate – if not shot in the meantime."

"He would be interested to know that his elder daughter behaved with less decorum than a common whore."

At these words she flinched and the anger she felt flashed across her face.

He laughed. "I think perhaps your father would also have you banished to a convent, or an asylum, if he knew what had passed between us."

In her mind's eye, Charlotte found herself thinking about the time when she had flirted shamelessly with this man, when she had deliberately sought to share his bed. The passionate moments replayed in her mind as she looked at him now and she knew that she still found him attractive. That given a chance she would submit herself to him again. "I just want to find an amicable agreement between us, so that the others do not have to suffer hurt or shame because of us," she blurted this out in half whisper, fearful that one of the servants may overhear them.

"Please don't concern yourself any further," he said to end their encounter, "I shall say nothing and will be politeness itself when we are in public together." Resting his hand on the door handle, he added, "But be warned that it is foolish to play games with me, Charlotte. You have done that once before and know the consequences of toying with me." He opened the door and smiled less anyone should pass and see them. "Good day, Charlotte, I have everything I need and shall look forward to seeing you at dinner this evening." With that she left and he gently closed the door behind her.

Slumping into a chair by his flickering fire, he wondered why he had ever been so foolish as to get involved with her. It must have taken vast amounts of alcohol to even become a possibility. Whatever, he had regretted the action even before it was over and cursed himself for being such a bloody fool! He had had no idea that she was even remotely connected to his friend Lovell. That just made the pain and stupidity of it even worse to bear. He must never find out about this whatever happened.

Nicholai was jolted out of these thoughts by a sharp knocking at the door. He shouted to enter and Andrews the butler entered and wanted to arrange for his bath to be filled. He agreed and two footmen entered with large jugs of hot water and proceeded to carry them through to his bathing room, adjacent to the bedroom.

"I have lit the fire in the bathroom, Count Romanov," announced Andrews, adding, "would you require a valet to attend you in the bath and help you dress, sir?"

"No, no, that will be all. Thank you, Andrews."

"There are two jugs of cold water by the bath, sir. If you need more hot, please just pull the bell cord and we shall attend presently."

"Thank you."

Nicholai watched as Andrews and the footmen left and closed the door behind them. He immediately stood in front of the fire and stripped off his clothing, glad to be free from the constraints of the fabrics. He looked at his reflection in the mirror and smiled to himself. He could see the sadness and emptiness in his own eyes, but knew that there was little he could do to ease his emptiness and salve his pain. Everything was now inevitable and even it if were not, there was nothing he could do to alter the way of the world and all the expectations placed upon those who lived within it. He just had to make the best of it and stop trying to create satisfactory resolutions to his problems where none existed. With that final thought he strode into the bathroom and poured a jug of the cold water into the hot water already steaming in the tub. Pouring himself a large vodka from his own hip flask, he sank into the warm water and savoured the moments of relaxation and silent contemplation of how life had brought him to this point. The road ahead was unclear. A new adventure, he thought. A new adventure indeed; he felt he was beginning to tire of the relentless conundrum that was his life.

Charlotte had returned to her bedroom and was glad to close the door behind her and for the privacy it offered. In the familiarity of her room she was able to vent her fury and frustration at her meeting with Nicholai. She couldn't believe that she could have been so foolish and had been blind to the fact that Nicholai was the friend of my betrothed. That she had enjoyed the chase and had flirted with him outrageously was of little consequence to her. She was more annoyed that these separate and secret elements of her life had crossed and caused the possibility for such embarrassment and, should it become known that their association had strayed into forbidden territory, it would undoubtedly explode and destroy lives and reputations – including her own!

As she prepared for her bath and decided what she would wear for the formal dinner that evening, Charlotte recalled with a physical shudder how disastrous that dalliance had been. It intrigued her that Nicholai seemed virile and handsome in his sly looks and half smiles during the flirtation that night. His initial passion once they met in her suite quickly became something confusing and disconcerting. Once he had stripped himself and her of clothes, he was like a man possessed as he threw her onto the bed. There was something of the animal about him, but at the same time a naivety that belied his rough actions. Suddenly, without warning, his ardour was halted and he became introverted. Silent. She responded by laughing at him. His behaviour was so odd that laughter was the only thing that she felt able to do in reaction to this sudden withdrawing of his virility, a virility that was a sham. Her laughter now seemed to echo in her mind. A smile spread across her face at the thought of his humiliation. She was glad and enjoyed his mortification at his own shortcomings; shortcomings that castrated him in her eyes. For all his handsomeness and virile body he was nothing but a masquerade of a man. She recalled a conversation they had months before at the Randolph, trying to analyse and make sense of it again.

"I do not have to explain myself to you," he said with a determined, defiant glare in his eyes, "not that you could ever understand..." She knew then that some dark, hidden demon of his had been revealed to her and he knew it. At this point it was not clear what that demon was, she thought in the moment, but it could be useful power over him to find out.

"What about me?" she replied haughtily. "Or am I an irrelevance to you in all this? Do I not have feelings too?"

"I have only known you a brief time," he said coldly, "but it has become clear to me that the predominant occupation of your thoughts is complete self-obsession." He paused as he looked at her with barely concealed disdain, before adding, "In spite of your charming, well-rehearsed, pretence."

"In which case," she replied getting up from the bed and putting a shawl around herself to cover her modesty, "I wonder why you ever contemplated our nocturnal liaison – as sordid as it is."

"A momentary lapse," he swiftly replied as he turned away from her as if her naked skin disturbed him, "in my usually accurate judgment of character." He gazed from the window, through the curtains, simply as a way of not having to look at her anymore as he hurriedly dressed. "No doubt aided by a large consumption of..."

"Vodka?" Charlotte spat back at him, infuriated that he could be so indifferent as to turn his back and his gaze from her in such an unchivalrous way. "It is unfortunate how quickly a man's ardour wanes as the effect of liquor wares off. It reflects the failings of any man at such times." His stillness and lack of immediate response riled her more. "Thanks to your inability, sir, I have endured a less than satisfactory night. It could not have escaped your notice but my admirers were numerous last evening!"

He turned and laughed in her face coldly. "No doubt, when another opportunity arises, you will find time to satisfy each and every one of them." His face became impassive as if trying to suppress his disgust at what was before him. "If you will excuse me now as this conversation, and you, are causing me great offence and are distasteful in the extreme."

With that final cutting remark he swiftly left her room and was gone. She raged and even shed a slight tear at his departure but more for the loss of what he could have been to her. He was a great suitor and much admired but it was obvious even to her that his personal and private personas were very different. The charm soon slipped away to reveal an aggressive and abusive nature in the man, handsome as he was. She would get to bottom of his mystery – of that she was determined.

Charlotte was jolted back to the task in hand as she looked over her chosen outfit for that evening's dinner party and was satisfied with what she had selected. She had little time for much fussing where clothes were concerned but she wanted to look her best. As she slipped into her hot bath water, she luxuriated in another secret and giggled to herself at how shocked everyone would be at its discovery. She smiled as she remembered the passionate sex she enjoyed with the stable groom, Rodgers, in the hayloft and also in the attics of the manor. He was rough, indelicate and very masculine in his dominating lovemaking. It suited her and made her feel alive. She also enjoyed the power she held over him and savoured the thought of using her riding crop to encourage him to satisfy her more. The smell of him both repulsed and excited her in equal measure. Unlike Nicholai, he was a real man in her eyes. It suited her to manipulate him – he was needed to make sure everything was in place for her plan; his strength invaluable to move the trunk through the labyrinth of attic corridors to where she needed it. With that, she closed her eyes, relaxed and luxuriated in her warm bath.

The convoluted relationships between my sister, Nicholai and Lovell, let alone the stable groom, I was oblivious to at the time. I had no idea she had even met Nicholai prior to his arrival at Willow Manor for my wedding. There were things about my sister I knew little or nothing about at that time and it pains me now to see the truth of the story. It is unbelievable to me that she could have been so adept at deception – both morally and with those she should have loved the most.

Dinner that evening was a beautiful memory to me. I remember singing whilst accompanied at the piano by Father. I had chosen the aria Softly Awakes My Heart, from an opera work by Saint Saens called Samson & Delilah that had become so very popular. It seemed appropriate for the occasion was the moment my heart would be awakening, in preparation for my wedding the following day on Christmas Eve. It was also a favourite of Father's, one he had asked me to learn because he loved its gentle, melancholy melody so. It is only now I wonder if it also reminded him of Mother, wishing that her heart would awake softly after all the years since it stopped beating.

As I sang, the warm glow from the candlelight illuminated the gathered company and added to the broad smile on Father's face. Charlotte was there beside him, her face also aglow but with time and hindsight I realize perhaps it was not as genuine as I thought.

I curse my stupidity and utter naivety and believe that if I had looked deeper and questioned her actions and behaviour more thoroughly, I may have been able to prevent the tragedy that was by then in motion. A drop more oil was added to the wheels of fate it would seem. As I look back and convey this story to you, it is more apparent than ever.

There were other things that, had I been more worldly wise, I would have questioned at the time. It wasn't just Charlotte, but also Lovell, and even Nicholai. Perhaps even Father, who I loved and protected with my whole heart, was less than open and honest with me about his life and actions? However, I was blind to it all and enveloped into a world where I trusted everything and everyone and didn't analyse the behaviour or motives of others. Why would I? I understand if you think me a complete and utter fool.

As I sang that night and watched the admiring faces I was lost already into the hands of fate. Through the tall, French polished, double doors that led to the hallway, I could see the grand staircase and the blazing chandelier that illuminated with its warm, soft candlelight. Lovell descended the stairs first and he seemed to catch his breath as he caught sight of me from the foot of the stairs. Slowly, with joyful eyes, he crossed to the doorway to watch and listen as I sang.

"Softly awakes my heart,
As the flowers awaken.
You love, tender as ever.

Now will I be forsaken,
Speak again, or sleep forever?
Oh say that from the heart,
You will never depart?

Thou so dear to my heart,

Thou so dear to my heart...

Moments later, Nicholai descended the stairs and he paused and smiled as he looked at me from the same spot. Slowly he walked up behind Lovell and then eventually rested his arm on his shoulder. In this position they watched and listened with rapt attention. Behind them I caught sight of Florence. She seemed disturbed somehow. As if she had seen something that had upset her. When she saw me looking at her she nodded encouragement and smiled brightly, as if she guessed I might have seen that look of concern.

> *Oh, once again, I implore thee!*
> *Oh, once again, say you adore me?*
>
> *I implore thee, say you adore me?*
> *Oh, once again, say you adore me!*
>
> *Spring wilt away,*
> *Gentle moving,*
> *So says my trembling heart,*
> *So loving, in its flight is not swifter than I*
> *When leaving all behind.*
> *To your arms I fly, into your arms I fly!*
>
> *Sunset, sunset,*
> *I adore thee!"*

That is all I remember from the time. Now I realize that Florence witnessed a small, covert act of intimacy between Lovell and Nicholai that disturbed her. She had watched as he slowly ran his fingers up Lovell's back before resting his hand on his shoulder. That seemingly insignificant action had other connotations for the worldly-wise Florence.

Later we were gathering to go through to dinner, awaiting the signal from Andrews that all was ready. As I passed through to the dining room with Father, I could see Millie lighting the last of the candles on the table candelabras, using a long taper. She was effective with her technique and managed to complete her task without any wax dripping from the taper onto the linen table cover. I recall the look of triumph on her face and a sense of pride at a job well executed. It struck me at the time that it took so little to create a sense of accomplishment in the house servants. Where would we have been without them? The candles were then lit on the Christmas tree in the corner, itself also garlanded with mistletoe for the occasion.

"This is one of the happiest occasions of my life," said Father with a depth of love in his eyes. "Your mother would have been so proud and would have wanted to be here so much." He suddenly struggled to retain his composure, the tears started to fill his eyes. "I know you will be happy with Lord Lovell. He is a good man and will give you a good marriage."

"Thank you, Father," I replied with a reassuring smile. "I love Lovell with all my heart and know he loves me. In that we are blessed. I just wish…"

"What do you wish, Ellen?" he asked with sudden concern. "You can always tell me everything, you know that don't you. What worries you?"

"I wish Charlotte could find a similar happiness, that is all. Sometimes I worry that she resents my marriage because I am younger." His expression changed to one of anger suddenly. "It is nothing she has said or done, Father," I hastily added in case he should think Charlotte had complained in some way, " it is just my sincere wish for her future happiness."

"Please don't concern yourself with your sister's welfare. I will make sure as a dutiful father that her future will be a happy one. Indeed," he added with a smile, "just because you are to be married doesn't mean you will never see her again. You will always be there for her, I am sure."

"Of course, Father, you are right," I replied with a reassured smile. "It just seems such a big change in our lives, my marriage, but it only adds to the family happiness and doesn't take anything from it. I see that now. Thank you, Father."

The footmen opened the double doors into the hallway with a nod from Father. He again seemed delighted and almost childlike in his pride for the occasion and me. His face beamed and his eyes sparkled so. That is the look I carry with me always; my most treasured memory of my beloved parent.

The assembled company began to cross the hallway from the drawing room, and then enter the dining room where they were directed to their seats by Andrews and Florence. It seems odd to say this, but I have no real recall of the names of those who attended other than my immediate family. They were friends of Father's and the family but their significance is now lost on me. Perhaps that is because they were not an integral part of this story and were not directly involved in the events leading up to my death. They had lovely smiling faces, faces I can still see vividly, dressed in their finest, and words of warm wishes, but other than that they have faded to mist in my memory.

My aunt, from the outset, I remember, commandeered Nicholai. She seemed to enjoy flirting with him shamelessly but only in fun. He responded in a similarly good-humoured way. She also enjoyed making Charlotte feel disconcerted by the fact, perhaps because she had the notion that Charlotte had eyes for the handsome Russian Count! Little did she know!

"In my experience," exclaimed my aunt to Charlotte whilst grasping Nicholai's arm determinedly, "dinner parties can be so dreadfully dull. Wouldn't you agree, Charlotte?"

"It altogether depends on one's company, aunt!" She indicated to the dining room. "Shall we?" She smiled sweetly as she made her way past them and into the hallway alone.

"I am sure, Nicholai, you would much prefer Charlotte

adorning your arm?"

"Only to deprive myself of such delightful company," he said laughingly, "I think perhaps not..."

"Why, Count Romanov," she replied coyly, "I do believe you are flirting with me?"

"Who, madam, am I to resist such an opportunity?"

At this they laughed as conspirators would. They were comfortable in each other's company and knew where any boundaries lay as a foundation for their mutual fun and enjoyment.

"Time my cousin dragged this place into the modern age," she said as she looked disapprovingly at all the lighted candles in chandeliers and wall sconces. "We cannot live in the dark ages and must embrace change."

"Excuse me?"

"My dear Nicholai," she replied aghast, "electric lighting! All these candles are positively lethal." She smiled at his bemused expression. Her eyes sparkling.

"No more dangerous than mature aristocratic ladies who shamelessly dazzle young Russian Counts with their considerable charms."

My aunt and Nicholai laughed delightedly and entered the dining room. Andrews showed them to their respective seats.

The next thing I remember of that dinner party was the conversation afterwards – and not without some irony considering what happened to me. For some reason the talk had turned to matters of the afterlife and spiritual beliefs. I remember this vividly as it was a subject that my father disapproved of – and one that equally fascinated my aunt, Lady Marlborough.

"My father has an aversion to anything the least spiritual," said Charlotte, "isn't that right, Father?"

"Typical," said my aunt with a hint of exasperation in her voice, "only ever to believe what one is capable of touching or seeing."

"We are all," said my father sternly, "entitled to our own opinion on such matters, Constance!" The company laughed more from nervous expectation than anything, but I remember it because I had never heard my father utter my aunt's actual name before in company. He always preferred the more formal address of Lady Marlborough.

"Nicholai," Charlotte said earnestly, "we would all love to hear your story – in spite of Father."

"I wouldn't want to offend you, sir…"

"It seems I am outnumbered, Nicholai," said Father with a resigned smile, "please tell them your story and I promise I shall not be offended by it."

"Thank you, sir." Nicholai then looked at the expectant faces all waiting for him to speak. He smiled and savoured the moment to add some drama. After scanning their expectant eyes he began. "In Russia, especially the Imperial Court, the looking glass is understood to hold mystical powers – it is believed that when you look into them, they can capture an essence of one's soul."

"What a ridiculous notion!" Father said before he could prevent himself. "It seems no different to how native African tribes reacted to cameras, when they were used to photograph them by missionaries, I understand."

"Richard," my aunt exclaimed with irritation, "let him finish!"

"So, in the Winter Palace at St Petersburg," Nicholai continued, "there is a special robing room. In that room is a full length, gilded mirror that once belonged to Catherine The Great – one of Russia's most powerful and ruthless Empresses." He scanned their faces to make sure they had absorbed his words. He noticed the candlelight sparkling in the wide eyes fixed on him, willing him to continue. "It has only ever seen the reflections of Russia's Empresses or Tsarinas in their Coronation or Wedding robes."

Lovell had also been as transfixed, although more by Nicholai's story-telling skills than by the story itself. His admiration for his friend was clear for us all to see if we chose to look. "Why?" he asked suddenly. "Why does it see only their reflections?"

"It is considered to bring good fortune. It enables the spirits of past Empresses and Tsarinas to pass good luck to their successor." After a pause he then spoke suddenly, making us all jump out of our skins. "But! Should anyone else dare to look at their reflection in the glass, the spell will be broken and luck changed. The penalty for doing so is immediate execution."

"With the greatest respect, Nicholai," said Father, "it does sound a fanciful tale…"

"I swear to you all gathered here tonight that I speak the truth."

"Oh, dear," said my aunt with a visible shudder. "It will make me shiver every time I look at my own reflection in the glass – more than it does already!"

"Do you really believe," I asked Nicholai, "that a looking glass has these mystical powers?"

"Yes," he replied without a moment's hesitation. His voice set and determined as if he was somehow displeased by the doubt of some. "I also believe that there are many things we do not understand in life and death. After all, every race and country has its own traditions and spiritual beliefs. Perhaps when you believe in something absolutely, it then becomes a truth?"

"It is no more extraordinary," interjected my aunt, "than those who believe the existence of an afterlife." The fact her comment created a silence, where everyone looked at her thoughtfully, amused her more than the pleasure she derived from the disapproving look on my father's face.

I was then the next to speak which, in light of my usual reticence for making myself the centre of any conversation, surprised the company more than my aunt's comments. "Or people who believe in the power of love?" With this I found myself staring at Lovell, who seemed to be embarrassed by my overtness and blushed a bright red in response. His reaction elicited a mildly amused smile from Nicholai, who also seemed to enjoy Lovell's embarrassment at my comment. Charlotte broke the silence, thankfully, and helped me recompose myself.

"If you would excuse me for a moment," she announced directly at Father, who nodded his permission for her to leave the table, "I need some air."

"Is everything alright, Charlotte," said Father, "are you ill?"

"No, I just have a slight headache and need to take some powders." She scanned the concerned faces looking in her direction. "Please don't be concerned, it is probably all the excitement of having company." With that she left the room and the footman closed the door behind her softly.

"Have you ever attended a séance, Nicholai?" inquired my aunt, bringing instantly the attention back to the subject she was determined would not be abandoned in light of Charlotte's dramatic exit. "I am reliably informed that even Queen Victoria indulges," adding as an aside to Nicholai, "she speaks to Prince Albert on a weekly basis!"

"Please, Constance, you go too far!" said Father, adding, "You know I do not approve of séances and all that nonsense – nor do I wish to hear about it."

Lovell then cut in directly and said to Father, "Excuse us Baron, Nicholai is sure to enliven any dinner party with some kind of contentious subject. He means no harm, I'm sure."

"My apologies, sir," said Nicholai to Father, "I am your guest and did not mean to take advantage or dominate the subject of conversation." He smiled at Father, but at the same time could see the sparkle in my aunt's eyes, as she suppressed an amused giggle at what she considered to be delicious mischief and highly entertaining.

"What tosh! Of course he's not offended," said aunt, "are you Richard?" She glared at him in a way that only she could ever get away with and within seconds my father acquiesced to her as he always did. A glimmer of a smile faintly rippled across his face, one that he quickly controlled to make sure she didn't get too much satisfaction from his climb down.

As this was going on, way up in the attic, Charlotte was pulling the old linen chest a few feet into its final position, adjacent to a short flight of service stairs near to the main bedroom corridor, as she had planned, and where she had instructed the stable groom to leave it.

She lifted the lid and looked at the interior. It was lined with a faded silk that had a few moth eaten patches in the lower corners. Its brass hinges were dulled with the lack of cleaning and it smelt musty and slightly damp. She screwed up her face and her nostrils twitched at the unpleasant smell that invaded them. She smiled to herself and then abruptly closed down the lid. She jumped at the heavy bang it made and then instinctively held her breath and waited a few seconds in silence, in case anyone had heard and came running. She exhaled with relief, and her breath seemed endless as it whistled past her teeth. Licking her dry lips she hurriedly went down the stairs to the main corridor, ready to join the rest of us again in the drawing room below.

Little did I realize it then, but time was quickly running out for me, Lovell and Nicholai.

Chapter 5

Reunited – Christmas Present
– December 23rd

Here are times when I find telling you this too painful. Sometimes I think I would have preferred to have remained oblivious to the convolutions and betrayals – but console myself by the fact I had to have all the information for a reason. They passed through my conscious thoughts like one's life flashing before one's eyes at the moment of death. At least that is what I imagined. I experienced no death as such, at least not one I remember, as my soul remained bound, as you know, to Willow Manor and its grounds. It is now possible for me to tell you everything that happened, even the parts I was not privy to in life in the past, or in spirit in the present. To understand, be finally free and be allowed to soar beyond this, I needed to know everything. Telling you my story is part of that release.

Christmas in the present day is a place that leaves me bewildered. The respect and dignity afforded to the Church and the celebration of Christ's birth has been sadly discarded in favour of what I can only describe as spiritual ignorance, avariciousness and the pursuit of personal pleasures. Religion and Christianity seem to have almost no relevance, and even less respect, to those who live in this time. I can see why my sister Charlotte, reborn to live another life in this present day, has found a place where she fits comfortably into this vortex of disrespect and disenchantment. There seems to be scant regard or dignity afforded to very much at all, apart from wanton greed and selfish endeavours. These are reflected back to these unfortunate people through strange, flashing screens, positioned as furniture or instruments held in their hands where other, somewhat disconnected people are seen or heard talking out at them. Many also talk to these instruments rather than hold conversations with each other. It pleases me that I was spared any part of this kind of life as living flesh. I should have hated it.

Charlotte and Nicholai had arrived at Oxford's Randolph Hotel in their carriage, after their first and traumatic experience in the derelict rooms of Willow Manor. Charlotte had recovered her composure and also managed, with the use of her mouth sprays, to control her breathing once again to near normal levels. However, observing her made me see that it had done little to improve her irascible and rude behaviour towards Nicholai. Why he tolerated such insolence from her was also a puzzle, but again, an attitude among women towards men that seemed oddly acceptable in this strange time that is now.

True to form, Charlotte had told Nicholai that she would not be able to stay at the hotel that night because she had to return to London on urgent business, to do with plans for Willow Manor and its future. At the time I found this puzzling, as I could not conceive a future for my home that did not involve restoring it and making it a family residence once again. However, even if it was with less than good grace, he accepted this and reluctantly waved her off from the hotel with a smile of sorts. Content it seemed, to await her return the following day.

It fascinated me to be able to watch him without him even knowing I was there. For me it was a progression of sorts because I discovered that after their arrival at Willow Manor that day, I was able to leave the confines of the grounds and travel further than ever before, but only in their company. My spirit was no longer trapped.

Once I had gained this added freedom, I also discovered that I recognized other faces from my past life but they were not reincarnations of the same people. Or at least if they were, they seemed unaware of it. Several of the staff at the Randolph Hotel I recognized as former servants from Willow Manor in 1893. It was perplexing until I was able to reassure myself that they were unable to see or hear me, I remember being fascinated by a woman at the hotel who resembled Florence and as I stared at her, she seemed to turn abruptly as if she could feel I was standing next to her. Her eyes were fixed, then confused and puzzled at finding nothing there to focus on and see. When I attempted to touch her gently, she flinched slightly as if caught by a sudden, unexpected breeze. But it wasn't Florence, not my Florence of the past; just a woman of a similar age, who happened to resemble her, but without her personality. It upset me, I remember, more than I expected. Dear Florence, how I missed her comforting embrace and wise counsel.

I also wondered if only those with unresolved issues in their past life were reincarnated or remained trapped as spirits like myself. Maybe that was why they physically resembled people from my past but did not have their soul? I am still unsure and still wonder at the possibilities of this for the future that is yet to be. One thing is for sure, their reflections in a mirror were unchanged from their present incarnations – unlike those from the past whose reflections were their past incarnations on first sight; even to the clothes they had worn back in 1893, that made them familiar and recognizable to me.

Nicholai had in some ways changed beyond obvious recognition. His present day clothes were odd and his formality of stature was gone but it was his eyes that confirmed the soul was the same. His eyes were a window to the past, the same little fleck of brown in the white of one eye, and the same kindness as before. His physique was still strong and he had the same dark hair but without beard or moustache. If he had dressed himself in his old naval uniform, as his reflection had briefly shown me at the derelict Willow Manor, the one he wore as best man at my wedding, he would have transformed back into the Nicholai of old.

I tried to touch his hand but it was impossible. He sat in the chair of his sparse hotel bedroom and dozed off into a light sleep.

Seeing his face in relaxed beauty stirred my heart and I so wanted to be able to communicate with him again, to let him know I was with him and how full my heart was at finding him again – and my hope he would bring Lovell to me. I slowly reached across and placed my hand on top of his as it rested on the arm of the chair. As I did so he seemed to smile slightly and the warmth of perhaps recognition spread across his face, that in life would have induced a tear to form in the corner of my eye. I held my withered hand thus, draped in the festered remnants of my bridal gown but could feel nothing of the warm flesh of his living hand beneath mine. I was immune to my own coldness but something stirred and he awoke with a jolt and for an instant I could see the fear in his eyes. He jumped up and looked about the room as if sensing an intruder. He relaxed and then, inexplicably, he burst into sobs of tears. His sobs were heart wrenching to hear. He crossed to his wallet on a side table and opened it to look at a picture he obviously treasured. Placing it back down he vanished into an adjoining room. I crossed to his wallet and I gasped at what I saw. There was a picture of my darling, Lord Lovell. I silently screamed out his name.

In a flash, as had often happened, I was back in the attic of Willow Manor. The chest was before me and that terrible, terrible recurring vision unfolded again before my eyes. I could see the chest lid being beaten from within as if someone trapped was trying to open it. I cried at the agony and wretchedness of this nightmare. The sound of the chest lid slamming shut rever-berated through the manor again and again and again in rapid succession. "Why? Why are you doing this to me? What do you want from me?" As always the chest lid burst open and I walked forward to see an empty space and the ragged remnants of the silk lining. I walked slowly away down the attic corridor, my decayed dress scraping along the floor as the wind whistled through that barren space. By thought I willed myself back to the Randolph Hotel.

Nicholai had undressed and showered and immediately looked better. He came back into the bedroom from the adjoining bathroom and I initially flinched at his nakedness. His figure was firm and toned and his chest hair dark and tightly spread. The same dark hair spread to his abdomen and groin, thinning slightly as it covered his thighs and lower legs. He grabbed a towel and covered his modesty, much to my relief. However, I had felt no shame or embarrassment at seeing his naked form, as I would have done in life. Indeed, I had never seen a man naked before and immediately wondered if my darling Lovell had a similar body in his prime but covered with his fine blond hair? It was something I was never meant to discover in my own life, as our love was never consummated and certainly no sight of each other naked would have been thinkable – if at all.

It was these thoughts that brought back to mind the photograph Nicholai had of Lovell. Moving to the table where his wallet still lay, I was able to see that the image, so clear, I had seen of Lovell, was in fact an image of Lovell in this time and place. I could feel a surge, a definite tingle, rush through my spirit at what this discovery meant. Lovell was here in the present and must have been reincarnated. It meant that he was friends with Nicholai and probably knew Charley too. It would seem that we were being reunited, fate was drawing us together. Perhaps this would enable me to find peace with them and thus be set free from this loneliness. As my screams were silent, so now was my shriek of joy at the thought I would be free to spend eternity with my darling Lord Lovell. The possibility overwhelmed me.

A machine suddenly jolted me from my reverie by making a loud jangling sound. Another strange machine that Nicholai crossed the room to pick up and then began speaking into as if he were speaking to a person. It wasn't until I heard him speak Charley's name that I realized he must be somehow talking to her, without her being in the room with us. It seemed to be a similar devise to those mobile handheld instruments also used to speak with. At these moments I felt so confused and ignorant of the world around me in this present time.

"Look, Charley," he said, with an edge to his voice I recognized as suppressed annoyance, "I am fed up being here in this room alone. I was looking forward to spending our first night of the holiday together. Instead I find myself in limbo waiting for you to come back tomorrow – so I will head to the bar and drown them!"

He crossed and sat by the window as she made her excuses to him and I could see the sadness in his eyes. Her voice was slightly shrill and edged with impatience at his petulance.

"For God's sake, Nicky, I already explained and said I was sorry." She spat the words out and they echoed through the room as they left the machine in his hand. "You were fine when I left you a couple of hours ago, what's changed?

There was a short silence as he thought about his answer. His face seemed to process the information and his expression changed from anger to resignation, then indifference in the fleeting of a second or two. When he spoke again his voice was calmer, more controlled and slightly glacial. "Please don't take me for granted, Charley," he said with determined authority creeping into his tone, "there is only so much I can take of this. Just don't push me over that line."

"Or what?" I heard her reply like a shot from a rifle. "Or what will you do, Nicky?"

His face changed again and I recognized an expression I had seen once before on Nicholai's face in the past. Looking across the room I caught his reflection in the large mirror above the dressing table on the opposite side of the room. I gasped at what I saw. There was the reflection of Nicholai of 1893, strongly imposed over his reflection of the present. The former image much clearer and stronger – dominant in that moment. As I stared he looked into the mirror and I knew in an instant he could see me! His eyes recognized my decayed form and he recoiled in horror and disbelief at what he saw. Suddenly the reflection of the present day Nicholai became dominant once again. He turned from the mirror; sweat trickling down his brow, shaken at the sight of me briefly flashed before him through the mirror.

"Just get back here early tomorrow, Charley," he said at last with no sign of the confrontational tone to his voice. "I just want us to have a good time and enjoy the holiday." He seemed distracted and unsure of himself as he added, "You will drive me demented one of these days – and probably too far!"

"Go and have a drink in the bar. That will help you sleep and I'm sure you'll feel better in some company," said her voice coming from the machine in his hand, "have one for me and before you know it I will be with you again. Good night."

"Good night," he said with more enthusiasm than showed on his face. He clicked the instrument off and began to dress himself. As he did so, I understood that I had witnessed the spirit of his past life become more dominant. It was capable of taking control again and it also made me wonder what secrets would be revealed about the relationship Nicholai had had with Charlotte. There was a link between them in the past as well as the present. I could see that now. It must unravel and be revealed.

Once he had dressed, I watched as he crossed to the mirror and put out his hand towards it – as if trying to touch something. He looked intently like he wanted to reach inside the mirror. "Who are you," he finally said. "I feel I should know you somehow but don't know why." Instantly I knew he was reacting to that fleeting glimpse of my reflection. He had no fear in his voice, but was obviously troubled and confused. "Were you just a figment of my imagination?" he said sadly, "Can I help you? What do you want from me?" His hand slowly slipped away from the mirror and hung at his side. He then smiled at himself and added dryly, "You need a drink buster, and quick!" With that he picked up his wallet and keys and left the room.

Once he had gone I remained for a short while to gather my thoughts and to try and understand what kind of relationship Charley and Nicky had had in the past as Nicholai and Charlotte. Maybe this would be a key to understanding my own fate. Where was Lovell? Why hadn't I actually seen his reincarnated spirit in this present time?

During that evening Nicholai had spent some time in the hotel bar and had drunk quite a large quantity of alcohol. The barman was courteous and considerate but eventually became aware that Nicholai was very sad and unhappy with his present circumstances. I watched as he was eventually escorted to his room by a manager and helped onto the bed, where he collapsed into a drunken sleep without even undressing. This kind of misdemeanour would once have been unthinkable in polite society and behaviour that I felt Nicholai would never have stooped to or condoned in himself or others.

I found myself thinking how much better it had been to be sheltered in the derelict loneliness of Willow Manor. Although I had raged against being trapped there, it sheltered me from the ugliness of the world and the horror of present day realities. By thought I was back in the darkness of the empty drawing room. A cold, whistling wind blew through the barren rooms and reassured me with the familiar sense of emptiness and loss. If I listened really hard and remembered a time of long ago, I could just about hear in my mind a long past echo of forgotten laughter drift through from the gutted ballroom. Then I could hear the words to a song of long past, its lyrics carried on the icy wind through the empty manor:

"The Baron beheld with a father's pride,
His beautiful daughter, young Lovell's bride!
And she with her bright eyes seemed to be,
The star of the goodly company.

Oh, the Mistletoe Bough!
Oh, the Mistletoe Bride!"

Nicholai suddenly woke with a start and sat bolt upright on the bed. He looked across at the mirror on the opposite wall and could see the hideous reflection of my decomposed body swathed in the rank and mouldy remains of my wedding dress. He first heard himself scream and then through his sobs he was surprised to hear himself call out, "Ellen, is that you? Where are you, Ellen? What do you want from me?"

He then collapsed again, his body saturated with sweat. He drifted into unconsciousness still trying to understand why he had called out that name – as if by instinct. Who was Ellen? Ellen? Ellen? Whose voice sang that strange song?

"Oh, the Mistletoe Bough!
Oh, the Mistletoe Bride!"

Charlotte sat bolt up in bed and shuddered as she recalled the Mistletoe procession of last night and then the dreadful dinner that followed. She could still hear the voices of the estate children singing that ridiculous song as Father and I paraded along the drive as the servants handed me sprigs of mistletoe for luck. This was 1893 for God's sake! We had stood on the porch waving and smiling with what Charlotte decided was sickening sweetness – oblivious of the fact it was quite frankly ridiculous and embarrassing to behave so in front of the servants. How they must have laughed and mocked the family, she thought, once behind their cottage doors or in their attic quarters!

Oh, the Mistletoe Bough!
Oh, the Mistletoe Bride!

Chapter 6

Randolph Hotel Secrets
Christmas Present – December 23rd – 1am

Nickolai slumped against the wall in the Randolph Hotel's reception area waiting for the lift to arrive. The staff and some other guests had eyed him cautiously as he staggered past them. He had decided he was too drunk to climb the stairs. The Morse Bar waiter, along with his superior, the hotel's manager, had discreetly suggested he might like to retire to his room again as his behaviour was beginning to unsettle other guests. After sleeping off his first drinking session earlier that day, he'd returned for more once he had awoken. It was with some relief that he took that advice – apart from an expletive in Russian, muttered under his breath, that none could understand to be offended by.

As the door slid open, I followed Nicholai into the elevator. I was struck by the sadness and despair that flickered dimly in his eyes. Something was wrong, something I was unable to understand or even comprehend. I could, however, see the loneliness in his soul. I knew how that felt and could recognize it instantly. As the elevator door closed with a staggered clunk, it reminded me of the first time I had ever entered such a contraption in life. Then there were gates and shutters to close and an attendant to operate the machine. Now it seemed to have a life and thoughts of its own; indeed, it even had an odd, disjointed woman's voice telling us what floor we were arriving at and when the doors were opening or closing. No sign of formality or manners.

As the elevator moved up, Nickolai stared at his reflection in the mirrored walls and seemed suddenly angry with himself. He crashed his fist gently at the glass again and again, as if trying to hit himself. He saw his present incarnation, whilst I could only see him as he had been in 1893. Worst, was the sight of myself that I could barely look at for even a second – although thankfully he could not see me. I screamed silently in despair at my own decay. The lights in the carriage flickered and dimmed, then went out, obeying my thoughts, plunging us into darkness for a few seconds that seemed like hours. Finally the rude woman's voice announced the 3rd floor and that the door was opening. The lights flickered and came back on even brighter than before, and the doors slid apart with a juddering clunk.

Nickolai rushed to exit the elevator and crashed into a maid carrying towels in the corridor. The towels immediately flew into the air and scattered at the feet of the startled girl. I was struck at how pretty she was and that her face was somehow familiar to me. It then struck me that she looked exactly like Millie, our maid from long ago at Willow Manor. She had also been rather clumsy and had often earned the wrath of Father, Florence or Andrews for breakages or some such misdemeanour.

"I'm terribly sorry, sir!" she said politely, with a soft Irish brogue, and in a voice I also recognized as Millie's. "I should have been watching where I was going. Are you all right, sir?" She smiled brightly at Nicholai and helped him steady himself. "Are you unwell, sir?" she asked him with genuine concern.

"No, I am fine, thank you," he said. Nicholai stared at her and held her gaze for a few seconds. She immediately became embarrassed and started to blush furiously. "Have we met before?" he asked her, puzzled by her familiarity.

"Of course we have met before, sir. Remember, I serviced your room earlier this evening, just as you were going out to…" She seemed to think better of being too chatty with him, remembering no doubt the housekeeper's warning about being anything but professional with guests, so added, "To the restaurant for dinner."

Nicholai seemed to momentarily regain sobriety as he continued to hold her gaze, much to her consternation. "Yes, of course, how foolish of me. Forgive me," he said with a laugh, "it has been a rather long day – good night!"

"That's quite all right, sir. Good night, sir."

Nicholai broke her gaze and carried on down the corridor to his suite without another glance at her. She watched him go intently. She picked up her towels and walked on. In a mirror at the far end of the corridor I could see her reflection and to my shock it was that of Millie the maid of 1893. She looked in the mirror back at me and suddenly smiled brightly. "I know you are here," she said, "I cannot see you clearly, but I know you are here, Lady Ellen."

At that moment a couple came out of the elevator as the doors juddered open. Millie turned sharply and looked down the corridor. She then scurried off, as if she had seen my ghost. Which of course, she had. Somewhere close by, a door slammed with such force it jolted me back.

In an instant I was back in the dark, deserted attic of Willow Manor and knew that before me I would see the same old chest and hear the sound of the lid crashing closed over and over and over again, as it reverberated through the vast emptiness of the manor in the dead of night. I watched in horror as the chest jolted and banged as if something or someone were trapped inside. Like a recurring nightmare, I knew every second of the ordeal and knew it ended as the lid burst open and I would step forward and peer in to the empty chest. In the silence that always followed, the chill howling of the wind echoed and whistled through the nooks and crannies of the manor. The eerie sound exacerbated by the silence and stillness of the night. As I walked away in search of nothing and nobody, the sound of my mouldy skirts dragging across the floor seemed to somehow mock me in my loneliness. What did it mean and why did this nightmarish vision come to me over and over again?

Back at the Randolph by thought alone, I was standing in Nicholai's darkened bedroom. Only the street lamp outside illuminated the room as the tree branches, bereft of their leaves, created a strange mottled pattern across the walls that was somehow gently relaxing and hypnotic. He was asleep, the alcohol having done its work and numbed his sensitive emotions. In sleep he seemed so much more handsome and his face was free of those anxious and tense expressions. In sleep he looked relaxed and happy and had that strong, dignified face I knew from 1893.

"Where is my darling Lovell, Nicholai," I said in a whisper close to his ear. "Where is he? I have waited so long. I don't want to be left here alone any longer. Please help me, Nicholai! Please help me find Lovell."

I watched his breathing and remembered what the sensation was like to take breaths of fresh air. How I wished that were still possible for me. Air was all I was in some way. Nothing solid that others could touch, and I could certainly not touch anyone, even if I wanted to. I was as nothing, as if carried on the wind and breeze to endure my fate.

"Don't let Charlotte hurt you, Nicholai," I said without realizing I was going to. "You must be strong and control her or she will..." I wanted to add, "destroy you" but I felt it was too painful a thing to say about a beloved sister.

Nicholai stirred in his sleep and I could see a single tear escape the corner of his closed eye. Transfixed, I watched as it seemed to slide in slow motion down his cheek, impossibly holding its position for what seemed forever, until it continued its slow journey to his chin. It dangled there as I watched and then with his next breath it slowly dropped onto the pillow and disappeared into the linen. All done in silence. It struck me as impossibly beautiful and made me recall the joy and sadness of tears in my own life. Something until this moment I had long forgotten.

I crossed to the window and looked out towards the Ashmoleon Museum opposite. The night was quiet and not a soul or noisy carriage was adrift in the empty streets below. For that moment I could have believed it was 1893 and not the present. I stood at that window all night, watching nothing and listening to the steady breathing of Nicholai. How I wished I could find Lovell. Maybe Charlotte would bring him; somehow I knew that we had to all meet again and soon. I could almost hear myself singing that aria I had sung on the eve before my wedding so many years ago. My heart ached as the memory enveloped me again – my long dead voice serenaded me as it echoed from the past to this present moment of melancholy.

Now will I be forsaken?
Speak again, or sleep forever!
Oh, say that from the heart,
You will never depart!

Softly awakes my heart,
As the flowers awaken.
You Lovell, tender as ever…

Oh, once again I implore thee,
Oh, once again, say you adore me,
I implore thee say you adore me!
Oh, once again, say you adore me…

Charlotte arrived back at the Randolph from London the next morning. She pulled up to the main doors of the hotel in her horseless carriage and promptly threw a bunch of keys to the porter and entered the reception with that swagger of confidence I knew so well. If she could see me she would be shocked to know that I could read her soul. In spite of this, I could not find it in my heart to be angry with her. I viewed her as a wounded spirit in her past life, and in this one nothing had changed to heal her. For that reason I found pity in my heart for her and the desire to help her.

A short time later there was a loud knocking at the door to Nicholai's bedroom. Bang, bang, bang and still he did not stir from his deep sleep. The sound unnerved me and I dreaded being subjected to the terrible nightmare vision of the chest in Willow Manor's attic. Thankfully I was spared. Nicholai stirred, looked at the bedside clock, then scrambled from beneath the sheets to cross and open the door. Charlotte barged past him, her impatience at being kept waiting so obvious as to make the atmosphere become heavy and negative instantly. I made my exit, as I felt unable to deal with the aggression in Charlotte's manner.

As I moved unseen through the hotel, I came upon the woman who so resembled our darling Florence. I watched her as she attended to paperwork in her office. She seemed efficient in her role as housekeeper for the hotel. How I wished that I could sense she was a reincarnation of the past, as Millie the maid was, but she seemed oblivious to me, or my reflection in the mirror that hung full length on the door. Neither could I see any glimmer or spark of recognition of her past spirit in her eyes. She was methodical in her tasks and seemed to have the same warmth of character. "Help me, if it is you, Florence," I heard myself whisper to her, " help me to make sense of this and to find Lovell." She crossed and poured herself some tea from a pot, added milk, and then returned to sit at her desk. "Please come back to Willow Manor and help to set me free, Florence," I heard myself ask with a pitiful tone. "Father would want you to help me." Her expression never changed. I decided it was pointless; she was unaware of my existence – present or past.

Traveling out of her office on a breeze, I could feel my long suppressed anger rise at the hopelessness of my situation. A world where I was unseen and unheard by those I encountered, was impossible to bear in this place full of living people. At least at Willow Manor I could be alone and not reminded of them and their busy, bustling lives, however undesirable that life seemed compared to the one I had once enjoyed. As these thoughts raced through my mind, I encountered Millie carrying a room service tray, loaded with tea and other delights en route to some guest. I found myself whirring round her and screamed sharply in her ear, "Stupid girl!" I wrapped myself around her legs and she tripped, landed heavily on the floor just before the tray and its contents crashed about her with a dreadful cacophony of sounds. Florence came rushing from her office and looked bewildered at Millie. I waited, hoping that Florence would chastise the girl for her clumsiness, but she immediately rushed to help her. It was then I noticed that Millie had a nasty gash above her eye that was bleeding badly. By this time others had responded to the noise and were helping her. I was shocked at my own spiteful and hateful behaviour, behaviour that I recognized as my sister's and not my own. What was happening to me, I wondered. I was ashamed.

Later that evening I would discover things about the relationship between my sister and Nicholai, and also more shocking discoveries that would turn my whole world upside down and inside out. Nicholai and Charley were arguing when I entered their room.

"You're a selfish, spoiled bitch!" said Nicholai from within the bathroom. "All you care about is yourself. You don't give a fuck about anything else, and never have if the truth be known."

Charley's face was strangely expressionless, as if she was really enjoying this confrontation. Nicholai couldn't see this, but there was the hint of a satisfied smirk on her face as she replied. "Up yours!" Under her breath she muttered, "how appropriate" the meaning of which escaped me in that moment.

"Go to hell!" was Nicholai's screamed reply. The aggression between them unnerved me, making me feel uneasy again.

Charley strode to the bathroom door and began banging on it hard. "Only twelve year old children lock themselves in bathrooms. Get back out here you son of a bitch!" She kicked the door in a sudden show of anger and cursed under her breath at the pain that shot through her foot and up her leg, as she didn't have shoes on. "Get back out here," she screeched, "and start behaving like a man – not an excuse for one! Bastard!"

Nicholai flung open the bathroom door and stormed out taking her a little off guard. Her defiant eyes were aflame with satisfaction because she had provoked such a reaction from Nicholai – albeit a violent one. He grabbed her by the throat with one hand and pushed her back towards the bed and then down onto it. She struggled but at the same time seemed to be enjoying his actions. She laughed in his face and dug her nails into his bare shoulders. I watched transfixed as little rivulets of blood slowly oozed from the wounds.

He winced with pain and then looked at her intently for a moment, slowly releasing his grip on her throat. The edge of fear mixed with pleasure on her face slowly dissolved. He got up and looked at his hands, horrified at what he had just done. Slowly he sat on the edge of the bed, as far away from her as he could. Charley emitted a couple of stifled sobs but defiantly composed herself – not wanting him to see how shaken she really was.

"What's happening to me?" he said with hollowness in his voice. He reached out to touch her but she flinched as if disgusted by his touch.

"What the hell is wrong with you?" She spat the words out in disgust. "You look the same, Nicholai, but it's like you are suddenly a different person." She got up and looked in the mirror to check if there was any bruising. She stroked her neck whilst inspecting it for any signs of redness.

"Maybe I am," he said at last whilst looking at his reflection in the mirror, "maybe I am." He sat and stared at himself.

As I looked at his reflection, all I could see was Nicholai of 1893. Present day Nicholai was nowhere to be seen. His past incarnation seemed to be taking over.

"I forgot to tell you," he said almost as an afterthought, "Lovell is joining us for dinner tonight."

Charley turned abruptly and stared at him in horror. "What? What did you say?"

"Lovell is joining us for dinner." He looked away from the mirror and caught her startled eyes and locked onto them. "Do you have a problem with that?"

"No," she answered after a pause. "I am just surprised that's all. Especially after all the trouble..." She began to laugh uncontrollably, mockingly.

Nicholai stood and swore at her in Russian before storming off to the bathroom to finish getting himself ready and to bathe his shoulder wounds. I noticed a few spots of blood had dripped onto the clean white bedding. When she was alone, her laughter subsided and a look of bewildered concern spread over her face. It soon hardened into a stern expression. Dear Charlotte was still there inside Charley. She had learned nothing from her past life to bring to this one. She was lucky to have had the chance; I had not had one full life, let alone a chance at another!

The fact they had said Lovell's name shook me more than the violence I had witnessed between them. It was the first time I had heard his name said aloud by them since 1893 and it stirred feelings inside my soul that I had forgotten were possible. Tonight, at dinner in this hotel, I would see Lovell again for the first time since that terrible, tragic day in the summerhouse, when he had taken his own life and slipped away from me.

Moving down to the Morse Bar, I struggled to appreciate the dress people considered appropriate for a formal dinner in this strange time. The name given to this lounge was also a mystery to me. What or who is Morse? Why would a hotel name a lounge area using that name? The young man serving behind the bar was well groomed and efficient and reminded me of a footman from Willow Manor. I crossed to look from the window and was surprised to hear a piano playing Softly Awakes My Heart.

I drifted through the reception area to the formal dining room and immediately began to feel more at home as I surveyed the fine linens, china and crystal glassware that adorned the tables. Small groups were bathed in candlelight and the highly polished grand piano was positioned in the far corner and the magnificent chandeliers were lit with electric light but were somehow very dimmed, thereby creating a softer atmosphere that Father would have approved of. The headwaiter, dressed in formal white tie and black tails, stood erect and business-like at his rostrum by the door, as formal as any butler.

I stood at the window looking out to St Giles and beyond. The evening light gave the university building's honey coloured stone a special golden glow, that was so familiar and unchanged in the bewilderment of this present time. I found it comforting, and the gentle playing of the piano accompanied with the tinkle of fine china and conversation soothed me. It was then I saw him again for the first time, through the reflection in the window. He entered the dining room and spoke to the head waiter, who then directed him to a table. Transfixed I watched as Lovell strode across the room, stopping to talk to a man at a table.

"Lovell, how are you keeping?" asked the man in uniform. He had, from a certain angle, a look of my father but he lacked the handsomeness and warmth of his face. Nevertheless, the resemblance, for an instant, was enough to shock me. "What a surprise to see you here," he said to Lovell with an edge of unease to his voice.

"As well as can be expected, Field Marshall Forsyth," said Lovell with confidence, although a coldness to his voice belied his true feelings. "And yourself, sir?"

"I am quite well, Lovell." After a moment's uneasy pause, he added: "I am only sorry it had to be me who instigated your resignation, Lovell. It was nothing personal you understand?"

"Of course, sir. It never is." Lovell smiled at him determined to remain pleasant in the face of what he obviously considered rank hypocrisy – the coldness in his voice told me that. He would not allow the Field Marshall to see the pain behind his smile, at his past betrayal at the hands of this superior. After all these years I could see that and understand his body language and tone so well – as if it had been but yesterday when I last saw him.

The man, Forsyth, seemed a little embarrassed. His wife then gave him a look that suggested he end the conversation and turn his attention back to her. "I had better go. Nice to see you and take care of yourself, Lovell."

Lovell made no attempt to shake Forsyth's offered hand. Instead he smiled brightly, nodded his leave at Forsyth's wife and crossed to his own table. It was only then it occurred to me I shared a name with him – Forsyth. Perhaps they were related to Father's side by some distant branch of the family.

The waiter brought Lovell his drink and he looked around the restaurant and settled in to its relaxed atmosphere. After a few moments Nicholai and Charley entered and spoke to the head waiter. He indicated they cross to Lovell and escorted them to the table, pulling out the chair for Charley to sit on, but she stopped and chatted to the man Lovell had been in conversation with. Nicholai took his seat. Charley then joined them. Lovell kissed her hand formally – in a way that I would have expected of him.

"Hello, Lovell, how are you?" Charley looked at him and smiled easily at his slight discomfort on seeing her again. "You've hardly changed a bit."

"Hi, Charley," he said, returning her smile. " Hi, Nicholai, you look great tonight." Charley seemed rather disconcerted at what she felt was a negative response, one at her expense.

"Thanks for helping me out last night," replied Nicholai, much to the bemusement of Charley. "It was all a little embarrassing really." He laughed nervously.

"You didn't mention you had met last night, Nicholai?" She looked from one to the other as if an explanation was required.

Nothing much seemed forthcoming.

"I arrived last night and managed to get a little drunk in the bar," Lovell said rather gallantly. "Nicholai helped me to check in. We hardly managed to talk apart from exchanging a few pleasantries. It was nothing."

This was as much a shock to me as it was to Charlotte. I had not realized that they had met the previous night, but it must have been when I found myself back at Willow Manor. Time, as with most things for me, seemed to have little significance as it did in life. The atmosphere between the three of them seemed strained, I could only imagine what the cause of this was as nothing they had yet discussed gave me any clue to the reason for any ill feeling.

"Well, thanks for coming both of you," said Lovell.

I guessed as an attempt to move things on and diffuse the awkwardness of the situation.

"Would you like a drink? He could see the flash of hostile looks between them. At that moment the waiter arrived with an ice bucket and stand and three, fine, fluted glasses. "I ordered Champagne, I hope that is okay? I wanted to celebrate our reunion, and another happy occasion, I understand?"

He took the bottle from the waiter and filled their glasses along with his own. All the while he seemed determined to keep the atmosphere happy and light if at all possible. Poor Lovell, he would have made an excellent diplomat and he was so very handsome I could almost not bear the sight of him after so long. If only he knew I was there, if only he could have seen me and realized what I had become!

"Congratulations are in order," said Lovell, "I believe?" He looked at them both and raised his champagne flute. "To the happy couple!"

To say I was shocked to the core would have been to underestimate my feelings in this moment. If I had a voice that could be heard, I would have been speechless anyway!

"And you want me to be best man, according to Nicholai," he added a little nervously, slightly put off his stride by Charlotte's stern expression. "Congratulations and a toast to you both."

"To the happy couple," Nicholai said a little glumly. "It seems the die is cast at last."

My whole being seemed to swirl and entwine itself in confusion at this unexpected news. Shocking news. How could Nicholai even contemplate marriage to her? They were so ill suited and I had witnessed nothing but hostility between them. I was entirely at a loss. What happened next appalled me and confirmed my reservations at this proposed madness.

"Excuse me, I need the ladies room," said Charley. She stood and walked a few paces towards the door, heard Nicholai's sarcastic laughter, and then thought better of it. She crossed back to the table and Nicholai looked up at her after drinking back a full flute of Champagne. Charley punched him with such force that his nose burst open and he was thrown backwards to the floor, chair and all, with a terrible crash. The restaurant fell silent and all eyes were upon the spectacle. Her Uncle Forsyth and his wife stood in horror and stared at them. Charley then made graceful exit from the restaurant without as much as a glance back at them, swiftly followed by her uncle and his wife, no doubt to support her and check she was all right. If looks could kill the other restaurant patrons would have been as dead as me.

Slowly the other diners returned to their own conversations, embarrassed at what they had witnessed. It was remarkable how quickly things resumed to normal. Nicholai stood and picked up his chair and sat at the table again – dabbing blood from his nose with a handkerchief. Lovell filled their glasses.

"Do we have a problem?" asked Lovell slowly sipping his drink. "She seemed rather pissed, don't you think? You were quite rude."

Nicholai forced a laugh and smiled at him. "Don't worry, she won't be back."

"I see," said Lovell, "not a great start to your engagement, is it?"

Nicholai looked at him aghast. "Shit, I can't believe Forsyth was here, there will be hell to pay now. Just what I need!"

"Don't worry, he knows how difficult Charley can be. He gets the brunt of her anger too, I imagine."

"Fuck, Lovell. I'm not talking about Charley. I mean you! He's seen me with you and I told him I hadn't seen you since…since all that business and your resignation from the Air Force." Nicholai took another swig of champagne.

"You disappoint me, Nicholai," Lovell said in a flash, with real hurt in his voice. "I thought you had more integrity than that."

"That's not fair, Lovell…"

"And what happened to me is? You are a despicable, shit of a friend sometimes and it escapes me why I even bother with you."

"You don't understand, and never will. The Air Force is my life," Nicholai said defiantly, "and always will be."

"What about me and my life? Or are you implying your life is somehow worth more than mine?"

"No, of course not! But you had decided to leave – don't deny that because you told me – so it made no difference to you."

Lovell looked at him with dismay. "In all the time I have known you, I never had you down as a conceited, arrogant bastard. But you just proved me wrong." He took a swig of his drink as if for courage. "The sad thing is, it's people like you, the hypocrites, that made life impossible eventually for all of us in the services. Don't ask, don't tell, and all that crap. Bull shit!"

"So now it's all my fault?"

"Spare me the mock indignity, Nicholai!"

"You should never have tried to involve me, okay?"

"When are you going to face reality, Nicholai? The only person you are fooling, or running away from is yourself. Can't you see that?"

"It was a mistake, that's all."

"Really?"

Lovell was so direct and calm but forceful, I was at a loss as to what the conversation was referring to – although it was obviously something very serious indeed. It upset me greatly to watch helplessly as these two friends bickered and treated each other so harshly; and in a way I never witnessed them doing in that other life we all had so long ago.

"Jesus, Lovell, give it a rest will you," Nicholai spat out in a hushed tone so as not to attract undue attention. "Can't we just put it all behind us and start again?"

"You are so predictable. Whenever the conversation starts to get uncomfortably close to the bone, you try and close it down. No wonder Charley is fed up with you – and hates me. She probably has been led to believe it is all my fault."

"What?" Nicholai said as he poured himself another flute of champagne.

"If you can't be true to yourself, at least be honest with her. She deserves that much at least."

All this made my head spin in confusion. I was listening to their conversation but it made little sense to me. The sight of them clashing in temper as angry words were exchanged made the atmosphere tense and uneasy. Others in the restaurant seemed to be staring at them with obvious disapproval. This I could understand, there was a lack of manners and grace that would have been unbelievable in their previous incarnations. I was suddenly exhausted and needed to return to the familiar surroundings of the manor. Perhaps there I could think about the unfolding events and try and make sense of it all. For the first time I began to wish I had never seen any of them again. At least my desolation and confinement at Willow Manor had allowed me to revel in my beautiful memories of the past, in spite of the horror of the decay and loneliness. I wanted to cry. Cry loud and bitter tears and scream out my agony of frustration for all to hear.

By thought I was alone again at Willow Manor. The silence embraced me instantly and I was once again where I truly belonged. I was unsure I could carry on any longer, but what else could I do? What other option did I have? I could not take my own life, as that had already gone. I could not even find respite in sleep for a few hours. Ghosts don't sleep. We have no rest. My story must be told, dear reader, or I shall never be free.

Chapter 7

Silent Night - Willow Manor
– 23rd December – 1893

L ate that evening after dinner, Charlotte managed to conspire a meeting with Lovell, in the drawing room, over coffee. Father, my aunt, Lovell and myself were engaged in a conversation about the next day's arrangements, at the far end of the room. Obviously it will come as no shock for me to tell you, reader, that I had not the slightest idea at the depth of my sister's betrayal – nor was I privy to the details of the conversation at the time.

Whilst in our conversation, I remember how Nickolai was distracted and seemed preoccupied with something about his reflection in the mirror – he stared at himself intently and in a way that seemed odd at the time. At the far end of the room, out of earshot, I could see Charlotte was standing a few paces to one side of Lovell and seemed to my furtive glance rather awkward and unsure of herself. I remember that distinctly because it was so unusual. Charlotte could be many things – she was never unsure of herself and her importance and station in life was something she never questioned!

"You have no need to concern yourself," said Lovell, with an icy edge to his voice, "they will never know."

"What must you think of me?" Charlotte's manner was seemingly sincere and her voice faltered slightly. "My protestations and actions are sincere, I have not been myself, Lovell."

"Nor I!" he said rather too hastily and punctuated it without necessity, making it seem harsh, ungallant even. "I was, shamefully I confess it, angry with you and regretted my words. They were not that of a gentleman."

Charlotte flinched at his reply because his tone seemed

devoid of any real feeling or warmth. It felt like he could have been discussing the dreary details of a parish meeting, not the intricacies of complicated emotional liaisons. "Your lack of understanding of my plight," she finally managed to reply, "is surpassed only by your indifference, sir!"

"I meant no offence," he shot back at her instantly. "My reasons are personal and beyond comprehension to you, a woman."

Charlotte's complexion reddened, a sure sign that she was beginning to find Lovell's reaction to her insufferable. She wanted his attention and her real desire was to have him devote himself to her, and her alone.

"Do you not understand, Lovell?" she said in a forced whisper – her heart wanted to scream the words at him, but she knew that would have been impossible, as then her black heart and emotional manipulation would have been revealed to everyone gathered at the far end of the drawing room. "Tomorrow," she hissed at Lovell, "I shall find myself in love with my brother-in-law! Not something I wanted or envisaged ever happening to me." She fumbled for her handkerchief in her dress pocket and then stifled a stage sob of agony worthy of any actress, for dramatic effect. To punctuate her drama she dabbed her eye. The whole pointless accusations were of her own making.

It was at this point in the folly unfolding between them that my aunt, Lady Marlborough, sensed something was perhaps amiss and intervened by interrupting their conversation. This obviously caused Father, Nicholai and myself to focus our attention in their direction, albeit briefly as it turned out, dear reader. More's the pity now I know what was actually happening and being discussed with my fiancé and sister on the eve of our marriage!

"Are you quite well, Charlotte?" Boomed my aunt from her position at the far end of the room. "Do you require some assistance, dear?"

Lovell, to his credit and with hindsight much stupidity, covered the tracks of deceit well for my sister by interjecting without a moment's hesitation. "She is quite well, Lady Marlborough, just a little choked because of want of a drink after such a delightful dinner." He crossed and poured Charlotte a glass of water from the carafe and handed it to her. "There you are, my dear, that will alleviate your discomfort."

"Thank you, darling Lovell," replied my snake of a sister, her voice all charm and sweetness. "I am much obliged to you." She then turned and smiled towards us and added in our direction, "I am sorry to have alarmed you, I am quite well, just a dryness of the mouth and throat that made me cough a little. Ellen, please play us something beautiful on the piano."

This quick thinking pleased the gathered company and fool that I was; I meekly sat at the piano and began to play a gay waltz by Strauss. What a blind idiot I was and if I could have only known then the treachery directed at me so blatantly – designed with no other purpose but to destroy my happiness and Lovell's.

"Charlotte," said Lovell in a firm but stern voice now they were once again inconspicuous in their conversation, "I have made it clear to you before, when you have insisted on declaring your love for me, that I can only ever love you as a brother-in-law would love you. I love Ellen, and always have, and can only beg you to desist with this embarrassing assault for my attention. Attention that I can never give you because I do not love you in that way – and never will." He held her defiant gaze for a few seconds to let this finally sink in and register. "Look, dear Charlotte, and yes I will continue to address you as 'dear', simply because I believe this nonsense is not really from your true nature but has come to the surface because of the heightened emotions aroused in you because Ellen and I are to be married. I appreciate as the elder sister it must be hard for you, and I know your fate seems to be that of your father's wishes to be cared for in his dotage, but nevertheless, I do believe that you will find a real happiness and have a marriage and love of your own given time."

"When I think of what we could have achieved together, Lovell. You and I!" said my jealous sibling. "It is a travesty that you would marry my ninny of a sister and prefer her to me. She will always look beautiful and elegant on your arm, but she will never match the pleasure I could give you with complete abandon. Sometimes I think you feel more for Nicholai than for anyone else, including Ellen!"

"Charlotte, you go too far! Your behaviour towards me and the scorn you seem to have for your sister shocks me. Not to mention your casual and unwarranted attacks on my friend. I feel I no longer know you – nor want to if this is your idea of propriety. What has possessed you to pursue this unrequited affection for me? It is certainly not a response to any declarations I have ever made in your direction."

Nicholai chose this moment to make his way over to join them. Lovell, darling that he was, I know, reader, he was true in his affections for me – and loyalty itself to our love for each other. Lovell's final words to Charlotte were said with a bright smile on his face, enabling him to mask the fury he felt at her silly, spiteful and unnatural suggestions to him. "Charlotte, my dear, this conversation is at an end," he said firmly and finally, lest Nicholai heard them as he approached, "and I shall choose to forget you ever addressed me so, with such hurtful, unkind comments about me, Nicholai and your dear sister, who loves you. I have never given you the least encouragement to think such nonsense and never would I. I do not love you and never would. My heart and its attachments, believe me, are far too complex a matter for my own comprehension, but of this fact I am certain. I could never love you in that way!"

Lovell had already resigned himself to put it behind them and forget it ever was said. For him it was the only way to proceed and establish a future comfortable for them both to inhabit. Knowing Lovell as I did, his natural thought was to put it down to stress and the fact that Charlotte was grieved, as the elder sister, to have her younger sister marry before her. In aristocratic society that sometimes meant the life of a spinster lay in store for the elder sister. He felt sure that would not be the case where Charlotte was concerned. Had I known of her deception at the time, I would have gladly banished her to the fate of spinster of the parish – and well she would have deserved it!

As Nicholai arrived in their company, Charlotte made some excuse to leave the room and departed swiftly as I watched from my vantage point, playing the piano. Nicholai I remember poured himself and Lovell a drink and then they stood gazing across at me with reassuring smiles on their handsome faces. Andrews was attending to Father and some other guests, as they laughed and chatted happily by the roaring fire. Florence, I noticed leaving the room with a tray of used glasses, smiling reassuringly at me as she left. On glancing back in their direction, I noticed that Lovell and Nicholai were then deep in some conversation. Through the windows looking onto the formal garden, the curtains I recall had not been drawn at that late hour due to the occasion, I saw one of the estate servants, a stable groom, I thought, peering in from behind a tree – he quickly slipped from view, perhaps because he thought I had seen him. I made a mental note to speak to Florence about it. Estate servants were forbidden to use that side of the house when we had guests and only otherwise if they were assisting the gardener or making their way to the lake and parkland for riding.

Nicholai and Lovell, as I turned to look at them again, were still in deep conversation. It seemed serious by the expressions on their faces.

"Please be careful with Charlotte, Lovell. I have suspicions that she could be trouble for you and Ellen. I could not find myself able to trust her."

"You seem to know her better than I thought. Like you had met her before you came here. Is that so, Nicholai?"

"Perhaps so, my friend, but it was nothing but a fleeting encounter at the Randolph and as such of no great significance. However, I know from that that she cannot be trusted and will cause trouble. She seems to me emotionally immature and capable of evil."

"Evil? That's a bit strong, isn't it? I mean, I know she can say some odd things and throw her raw emotions openly at one – which in itself can be disconcerting – but evil is too much."

"Lovell, you can be so naive sometimes. But I imagine it is what I have always loved about you. Your nature is so loyal and trusting and you could not see evil if it announced itself with a calling card and a military brass band!"

"I am not that unworldly," replied Lovell with laughter escaping his throat, and nearly choking himself with his brandy. "I just try to see the good in people. Like I have with you, old friend. We have had our arguments, but things have worked out as they have meant to and how things should, considering life's expectations for us."

"Indeed, but you forget I am Russian, Lovell, we live life by different rules and do not restrict ourselves to the expectations of anyone or anything – even life's! That road leads to boredom, frustration and hell."

Nicholai, I found, often talked in puzzles, so much so that I always felt confused and a little irritated, in spite of my real liking and affection for him. Lovell never mentioned any such feelings of his own regarding Nicholai, but I did at times see something I assumed was doubt in his eyes, at his friend's behaviour and arrogance – and his familiarity and honesty could also shock. My aunt, of course, loved Nicholai and could see no wrong in him. Everything Russian was romantic and excusable!

Little attention was paid to Charlotte's absence, although

Father did ask Florence where she was, so had obviously realized she had left the company. None of us could but know it, but it was a time that she was using to develop her plans, refining them and making sure all was in place to set them in motion the following day after the wedding. I wonder if any of us were truly safe in our beds and little realized it at the time.

Florence had followed Charlotte out of the room, after Father's comments about her absence, and was quickly trying to establish where she had gone. She knew that she had been upset and had tried to watch and listen discreetly to the conversation between her and Lord Lovell, to no avail. However, she could see through the forced smiles and façade of politeness, to sense the sub-text of their conversation was laced with aggression. Lord Lovell had seemed genuinely angry, something she had never thought possible considering his easy humour and infinite patience. But then she knew only too well how difficult Charlotte could be and how demanding and spiteful, when she failed to get her own way. She had the battle scars to prove it where that was concerned.

Florence had quickly established that Charlotte had rampaged her way through the kitchens and staff as she made her way outside. She often used the servant's quarters when guests were at the manor, so she could avoid being seen in the public rooms. The staff had borne the brunt of her temper on too many occasions to count, and her sharp tongue and abrupt, often spiteful, behaviour made them scurry out of her firing line if they knew what was good for them. Thus the inevitable wake of devastation she left included, this time, a teary-eyed Millie, who had not managed to avoid Charlotte but had literally been knocked off her feet as she pushed her aside. This had resulted in a nasty bruise to her cheek. Florence was furious and felt her temper rising dangerously. Physical attacks she would not tolerate, and unless Charlotte apologized to Millie, she would this time report her violence to the Baron.

As for myself, as I look back and see the unpleasant creature my sister truly was (even now I find it hard to believe I can say that about her – it pains me still in spite of knowing the truth of the story) I feel desperate and shocked that I could have been so oblivious to her and her wickedness. If only I had been able to see the whole truth at the time, so much unhappiness could have been avoided, so much of my own desolate plight could have been prevented. Can you even begin to imagine how terrible it has been for me to have this terrible, harsh truth unravelled before me, so that I could pass it on to you? I feel at times that it is a torture to me to retell this tragedy (for indeed it was and still is) so matter of factly. Nevertheless, it is my fate to do it, so I shall continue to the conclusion.

Once she had stormed out of the kitchen, she had, according to the cook who informed Florence, made her way towards the stable block beyond the general carriage house and blacksmith workshops. Florence then decided to let her cool her temper with a brisk walk in the perishing cold air – and perishing it was! One's breath vaporized into white, steamy clouds with each exhaled lungful. She would soon return faced with the bitterness of the night.

Little did Florence, or any of us know, but Charlotte had sought comfort in the stable block, and more specifically, in the quarters of the stable groom who was helping her with her plans – although he would have been ignorant of her true intentions towards me. She enjoyed the smells and the earthiness of the stables and it made her feel alive. The smell of the coal fire in the small hearth and this powerful, rough man. She loved to watch as he crouched down rubbing his hands to benefit from the scant warmth in his freezing room. As she entered, he rose to his full height and smiled. In an instant he had crossed to her and grabbed her waist with his rough hands, with the intention of kissing her in his usual lustful manner; his instant arousal obvious as he pressed against her. He had misjudged her and she viciously slapped him across the face and pushed him away. For an instant he was unsure if this was part of the game she wanted prior to sex (yes, reader, sex) or if she was serious.

"Get your filthy hands off me," she said as she pushed past him and crossed to stand by his small fire. "How dare you presume to handle me in such a way without my permission. Know your place!" Fighting back a sob of despair, she quickly retained her composure. "This room is freezing, do you have more coal to burn?"

He laughed to himself and looked at her, still confused by her attitude. "No ma'am, we have only a small allowance of coal and my few lumps per night don't last long, ma'am."

"I will have to speak to Father, this is too cold a night and your allowance for heating this place clearly inadequate." She looked at him and could see he was still unsure of her. "I am sorry for striking you, you took me by surprise and I have had a terrible evening with one thing and another. I came here to elicit your help again, if you would be amenable and would forgive me?" She smiled weakly at him and sat on the stool beside the fire, making sure her dress didn't get dirty on the bare floor as she did so. "I am so unhappy. I didn't know where else to go and could only think of coming to see you – you are in a way my only friend and confidant here."

He searched her face, trying to see if this was some kind of game or a joke. He spat into the corner of the room to clear his mouth of a little blood that had resulted from the hard slap she had given him. He then crossed to a wooden chest and lifted it and took a couple of logs from it and placed them on the fire. He grabbed the poker and cleared the embers, making the flames lick around the logs, almost instantly creating sudden warmth that also filled the room with a heartening glow. The sound of the logs hissing and spitting were the only sounds until he spoke again.

"I am always at your service, Miss Charlotte. What is it you wanted of me, ma'am?" he asked as she stared into the fire, lost in her own thoughts, wondering what game she wanted him part of. "I am always grateful to you for...for everything and you knows that ma'am."

After a moment she turned to look at him and smiled. "I wonder?" she said a little mysteriously, and then giggled as she turned her face back to the fire.

"What?" he asked her, "what is it ma'am?"

"I wondered if you have ever killed a pig?" Her eyes lit up and then she added, "Slit its throat to stop it squealing and thrashing about?" She looked directly at him awaiting his reply. "Didn't you once work on the home farm here?"

He was aghast at first because she seemed to relish the idea and he couldn't quite work out where this was leading. "Why would you want to know about the killing of animals, ma'am, "he said warily. "It's not for you to think or worry about such things."

"Do they feel any pain once their throat is slit quickly?" she asked, with relish in her voice. "Does the knife have to be very sharp for this purpose?"

"Yes, ma'am, I suppose it would help if it were..."

"Especially if it had to be done so no commotion and screaming ensued," she asked seriously and rather chillingly, "so it wouldn't disturb anyone and make it obvious a pig had been killed. Is there an awful lot of blood to deal with?"

"Blood is terrible, but if you have a good bed of straw beneath the animal it doesn't be too messy, ma'am." He looked at her again, slightly startled by her line of questioning and also her glee in seeking the information and the answers he gave.

"I think you will be able to help me solve my problem. Would you be willing to help me again? It was a lot to ask, I know, getting you to move that big, heavy chest through the attics of the manor, and you did it so well and nobody is any the wiser of its new location." She smiled at him and stood to look into his eyes. "I have always shown my appreciation for your help, haven't I?"

"Yes, ma'am," he replied, with a sudden rush of expectation and blood to his loins.

"If you are careful to unhook me at the back," she said as she turned to give him access to her dress fastening," but I cannot be too long as I will be missed and will need to get back to the manor." She slipped her dress off and stretched out on his rough bunk of a bed and watched expectantly as he slowly slipped off his clothes and stood before her, naked in the firelight. His powerful frame dominated the room and excited her. As he crossed and lay on top of her she trembled at the thought of what she had decided to do. As he began to roughly take her, his masculine smell overpowered her and she whispered in his ear, "Do you have a sharp knife?"

"Yes, ma'am," he said, suddenly frozen. "Why do you ask me that?"

Tearing her nails into the flesh of his back, which made him thrust into her violently, she said, "Because I have a pig I want you to kill for me..." She shuddered at the power of his body domineering her and then whispered again in his ear, "A Russian pig!"

Florence was waiting and watching from the kitchen window, worried that Charlotte had not yet returned from her walk into the night. She was just considering getting her shawl and going out to search for her when she suddenly appeared, making her way back towards the manor. Sighing with relief she was about to go out and chastise her, when the drawing room command bell tinkled insistently and she knew that would have to wait until later, as she quickly made her way to the drawing room. She was aware by this time that there was something wrong with the relationships between Lovell and Charlotte and Lovell and Nicholai and was only certain that I was oblivious to it all – as was Father, of course. It was as if we were all being hurtled together along a trajectory of fate, that could not be stopped or rearranged by anyone. Florence was convinced there was trouble ahead.

Charlotte's hatred for Nicholai was less about his rejection of her and more about what she had discovered by accident about his relationship with Lovell. She had determined to speak to Lovell and attempt to seduce him, by way of a nocturnal visit to his room once everyone was asleep. What she had found shocked her and lit the flame of her irrational jealousy. Having crept along the corridor with only a candle for light, she managed to slip into Lovell's suite of rooms, via the valet's pass door to his bathroom, once entered she made her way easily into his bedroom chamber. She crossed to the bed quietly, intending to perhaps slip beneath the sheets with Lovell and excite him with her charms. The thought made her smile and catch a laugh that threatened to escape her throat and give her away. As she approached the bed she raised the candle to facilitate her view of his handsome features, only to be faced with something incomprehensible and beyond belief. There, in Lovell's arms, lay Nicholai. They slept embraced and content and it seemed that it was not something unusual to them. Charlotte caught the cry in her throat and suppressed it with much pain and hurriedly left the room by whence she came. Her heart beat erratically and fast and she struggled to get her breath once back in her own suite of rooms. Disbelief ricocheted back and forth in her head at what she had seen. Her hatred was now directed at us all – we were all to find ourselves victims of her irrational jealousy and calculated thoughts of revenge.

Florence had of course guessed this attachment between Lovell and Nicholai and had assumed that it was just a depth of friendship between them and was wholly innocent. Or at least that is what she preferred to let herself think, as the alternative was too difficult in its implications to even consider. Besides, she rationalized it by considering that they wouldn't be the first aristocratic men to have a boyhood attachment of affection, that ended once a marriage occurred for one of them. It was just the way it happened sometimes. She was sure that Lord Lovell loved me and that his intentions in marrying me were nothing but sincere and also as a result of love.

After Charlotte had worked her sexual charms on the stable groom, she had forged an arrangement with him for the following evening, after the wedding and in time for the traditional game of hide and seek that would be played as part of the marriage festivities. She would send Nicholai a note, seemingly from his lover, Lord Lovell, to meet him urgently in the old summerhouse by the lake at a certain time. Once Nicholai arrived, the groom would be waiting to ambush him and put to good use the sharp knife suitable for slaughtering pigs. It would be quick, clean and noiseless and his body could be wrapped in sacking, weighted with rocks, and flung into the lake. The groom was willing to do anything for Charlotte and he was completely manipulated by her and the power she held over him.

This grisly end for Nicholai would enable her to create a scenario involving me, that would appear to show that Nicholai and I had run away together to Russia, leaving a jilted Lovell to be comforted by a sympathetic sister in Charlotte. In her warped mind she truly believed this plan would enable her to have him for herself. Once we were removed, it would be simple for her to manipulate him to her advantage – or so she thought. That was all well and good – but what of me, dear reader? How was I to be disposed of, as Nicholai lay decapitated at the bottom of the lake?

That evening, back in the drawing room, my aunt, Lady Marlborough, had been doing her utmost to contrive a situation where she could engage Nicholai for a quiet conversation. A conversation that now leads me to believe that I alone, except Father, was the only one lost in a world of my own impending happiness, with little idea of the convolutions of the relationships around me. But more of that soon. Sitting at the piano I gaily played jolly waltzes and polkas to amuse, as the people I loved most in the world conspired to destroy each other and reveal their darkest secrets about each other, by accident or design. In that time, during my life, I would have found it hard to believe any of it, indeed I would never have thought that such things could happen or those I loved could behave in these ways behind closed doors. I was happy then in my ignorance, innocent of it all, but now, glad I understand the truth of it all in all its harshness and wretchedness. However painful, I need to bear it still for the sake of revealing the truth to you, dear reader. I find myself regarding you as more of a friend to me than a mere reader of my story. A friend you shall now be considered.

One happier moment of that evening I enjoyed enormously was a surprise that Father had secretly planned for me. He called us together around the piano to make his announcement, with a solemnity in his demeanour that I guessed would involve some mention of dear departed Mother. In his hand he had a leather bound Cartier box that was quite long, so, I thought at the time, far too large to hold a brooch or bracelet of some kind, but too narrow to contain any kind of tiara. That said, my expectations were still heightened considering the occasion.

"My dear friends, family and children," he began, and then suddenly realized that Charlotte was not in the gathered company. "Where the devil is Charlotte? Why does she always manage to disappear when most importantly needed," he muttered under his breath, more in exasperation than annoyance.

"She will not be far, cousin," said my aunt, glancing at Andrews who had crossed the room with a tray of prepared sherry filled glasses. "Could you find Miss Charlotte for us Andrews?" she requested of him as she took a glass of offered sherry from the tray held before her.

"Shall I go and ff-find her," announced Lovell, his stammer returning to add extra strain to the moment at hand. "I think she said she felt rather unwell and wanted some air…"

"I will go and ask Florence, sir," said Andrews, making sure everyone had a glass. "She will know where Miss Charlotte is, I am sure, sir."

"Be quick about it man!" said Father rather too abruptly. Just at this moment Charlotte burst into the room and seemed rather flushed, as if she had been running or escaping some phantom in pursuit of her tail. She quickly slowed her pace and regained some semblance of dignity, composure – and dare I say, decorum. Florence entered the room behind her and silently closed the doors.

"I am sorry, Father," she said full of sweetness and feigned innocence, "I had a slight headache and needed to take some powders and lay down for a short rest. I am quite recovered and apologize for my longer than expected absence." She then pulled a lace handkerchief from her dress pocket and gently dabbed her brow to remove the obvious perspiration. I noticed, though I doubt others did, that she had some rather odd dusty, dirty streaks on her silk gown. The folds of the silk, and the dark colour of the gown, helped to make them less obvious. She picked up her sherry glass, smiled at us all, then looked at Father with an expectant expression on her face.

"Lady Ellen, my beautiful daughter, on the eve of her marriage to Lord Lovell. Indeed, as you know, it is why we are gathered here this Christmas to celebrate the occasion and the season. Sadly my dear, darling wife, Ellen's mother, is not here to share this happy time but I hope perhaps she will be here in spirit, to join in the celebrations in some way." He paused as he looked at Mother's portrait hanging on the far wall, his eyes filling with tears. "So I would first like to ask you to raise your glasses and to drink to the memory of my wife." The assembled company all looked at Mother's portrait and raised their glasses in silent homage, then sipped the sherry within respectfully.

Nicholai, I noticed, seemed to find it all a bit strange, if not somewhat melancholy but then his natural good manners kicked in and he smiled and was charm itself. No doubt he considered that if he could talk about mystic mirrors and dead Tsarinas and Empresses of Russia, then his English host could pay tribute to his dead wife on the eve of his daughter's wedding, without seeing how that might cast a slight gloom on what should be a joyous, happy time.

"Some months ago," said Father earnestly, continuing, "whilst plans were being decided on for this wedding, and my daughter's wish to be a Mistletoe Bride, married on Christmas Eve, as was her mother to me, I decided to mark the occasion with a special gift." Father looked at me and smiled reassuringly as he knew I would allow the emotion of the moment to overwhelm me, as it usually did. "This gift is special because it will pass on the link between my wife's marriage to me and my daughter's wedding. I hope you will wear them with pride tomorrow, Ellen." Father then handed me the exquisite, red leather box that had a gilded monogram of the famous royal jeweller engraved into the leather.

To say I was speechless by the presentation of the said box would be an understatement. All I could do was look at Father and then at the faces of those around me. As I recall, Charlotte seemed to have a pinched and aloof expression on her face. Her eyes were cold and stared at the box rather than at me. Perhaps she knew what was in the box handed to me and was covetous of the contents? At the time I was so foolish as to be oblivious to such things. Lovell looked at me with warm, smiling eyes, and ever in the background, I could see dear Florence smiling reassuringly at me. The expectation in the air created stillness and a silence that was at the same time eerie but also laden with expectation. I remember hearing the gentle roar of the fire, and then as I lifted the lid of the box a collective gasp of delight and surprise. There, gently formed in a pink, silk lining lay the most beautiful string of pearls I had ever seen. It immediately made me look at the portrait of Mother on the far wall, and there she was wearing the very same pearls. Tears pricked my eyes and I was beyond containing myself at this gift from Father. He crossed to me and kissed my cheek, a rare show of affection in company, and one that shocked me as much as the gift itself. He took the pearls from their case and draped them around my neck, whilst expertly fastening the clasp.

Once everyone had finished their exclamations of delight and comments about the beauty and the quality of the pearls, Father once again commanded the attention of those present.

"May I propose a toast to the happy couple, Lord Lovell and my darling daughter, Lady Ellen Forsyth and wish them a glorious wedding day on the morrow, and a long and happy life together." Father paused a second for dramatic effect before adding somewhat mischievously, "Hopefully their union will be fruitful and bring us a son and heir for Willow Manor and the continuity of the baronetcy!"

Those assembled dutifully raised their glasses and sipped their sherry by way of courtesy and then Lovell asked me to play and sing Father's favourite aria, Softly Awakes My Heart, which I duly did and gladly. At that moment I would have done anything to please Father, as I know how hard it must have been to give me my dear Mother's pearls. As I began to play the intro-duction on the piano, I noticed that my aunt had finally managed to get the attention of Nicholai and they wandered to the far side of the drawing room, soon deep in conversation. Florence was talking to Charlotte by the main doors.

"Where are you going?" asked Florence as she saw Charlotte making her way towards the door. "You're not ill or anything?"

"No, just a little envious!" Her whispered tone surprised her with its bitterness, so she made light of the next sentence. "There is only so much happiness one can bear, especially other peoples."

"The one time your sister manages to attract attention away from you and this is your reaction?" Charlotte could see that Florence was angry with her. "I worry for your character sometimes, Charlotte. Your mother would be appalled."

Charlotte turned to look at Florence and made her eyes fill with tears. "I hate myself for it too, please don't be angry with me." Florence's expression said that her thoughts were that Charlotte could out perform any actress of the stage. But she could never say that outright, as it wasn't her place to do so.

"While we are having this discussion," added Florence, whilst she had the opportunity, "I suggest you keep out of the stable block and also choose to keep better company than Rodgers, the groom! If your father were to find out there would be trouble. Is that clear, Charlotte?"

Charlotte's face was suddenly frozen in shock. She swiftly moved away from Florence and came back to the piano where I was playing and singing to amuse. Charlotte was unsure how much Florence knew, how much she had guessed.

"Charlotte is a puzzle to me, Nicholai," whispered my aunt to him conspiratorially, "she seems so distracted and most of the time she seems elsewhere in her mind. I never know what to make of her mood swings."

"Forgive me, but I know little about her and have hardly made her acquaintance – not enough to be a fair judge in the matter. Whereas you have known her all her life?"

"Indeed I have, Nicholai, indeed I have." She looked at him kindly and smiled warmly in an attempt to put him at ease with their conversation. "What about you and Lovell? Believe me when I say your situation will become easier with time. You do know that?"

Nicholai was immediately caught off guard and was momentarily flustered. "I am sorry, I don't understand," he said. Her knowing smile told him his protestations were useless, nevertheless he carried on regardless, more from embarrassment. "We are friends and have been for a long time..."

"I may appear to be a foolish old woman," she said cutting in kindly, "but there is very little in this world that has ever escaped my notice." Her eyes were full of compassion as she added, "It is always better to depart with dignity – and good memories?"

"In this moment, nothing feels very dignified…"

"Be rational, Nicholai, leave here as soon as you can after the wedding tomorrow. Should your association with Lovell be discovered the reaction would be venomous – it is better for everyone, especially his bride, my niece. Please don't allow her to be hurt in all of this. Better she remains in ignorance."

"I have already made my decision," he said sadly. He then looked into the gilt mirror that sparkled and reflected the flickering warmth of the candlelight. The glow added a sepia tone to the view and seemed to embellish for the better the complexions of those caught in its reflection. "We look in the mirror and what exactly do we see?" he asked her somewhat mysteriously.

My aunt was confused, but answered him logically. "One's self?"

"Of course," said Nicholai, "but the image is reversed, the reflection in fact the opposite side of the same coin."

"I am not sure I understand?"

"Maybe we need to experience both sides of our character, to ever understand either?" He looked at her and smiled brightly. "Thank you for your advice, it is much appreciated and I know I will retain your confidence and discretion in this delicate matter?"

"Of course." She clasped his hand to her with affection. "My late husband gave me a wonderful life, but our marriage never eased his pain at not being able to live according to his true nature. My regret was never being able to have children. We were great friends and companions.

"You are very wise, madam!"

"Not according to stuffy English society and all its expectations and demands."

"Therefore I will ensure you are the talk of St Petersburg – the Winter Palace will echo with your name and the Tsar shall hear all about you and your kindness."

"Nicholai! I would die a happy woman at the very thought of it. Wait until I tell Lady Astor, she will be livid with jealousy!" She laughed delightedly and more so when Nicholai kissed her hand and bowed his respect to her.

"We better join the company before everyone retires for the night."

Nicholai offered my aunt his arm and then looked at me playing the piano with warm smiles and moved to where Father was sitting with Lovell by the fire.

To all intents and purposes it had been a perfect evening, one that had been on the surface so jolly and polite, with good company, music and the expectation of mine and Lovell's wedding the following day. In blissful ignorance of the darker goings on around me, I bade them all good night and contentedly retired to my room. Although tired I was still excited and couldn't wait for the pleasures the morrow would bring. My night was to pass in sleep, unlike others.

Just as dawn broke on December 24th, Lovell was standing naked at his bedroom window. He watched as in the distance Charlotte could be seen riding a large chestnut horse, with the stable groom on an equally powerful mount, as they galloped off over by the parklands, and the summerhouse barely visible amidst the swirling mist coming off the lake, from the valley beyond. The frost had covered everything and the landscape sparkled as the weak wintry sun began to rise.

Nicholai was in Lovell's bed asleep and awoke suddenly. Realizing Lovell was no longer beside him, he sat up and looked around, momentarily confused. As soon as he saw him standing by the window he relaxed. After a moment he climbed out of the bed quietly and joined Lovell by the window. He wrapped his arms around his waist from behind and looked out at the view with him.

"You're ice cold! How long have you been standing here?"

"I can't fight you anymore…"

"Let's not talk about it now."

"We must. Not seeing you for so long made me assume it was…was part of our boyish past, and that it would stay there. Somehow forgotten."

"I have never wanted anyone else, Lovell. I have felt an emptiness for so long without you…"

"Please, Nicholai, don't! Our situation is hopeless, why can't you see that?"

"We could leave here today. There must be somewhere we could go…"

"Where? It is not possible, besides I…"

Nicholai cut in and finished Lovell's sentence for him, "Love Ellen?" He smiled sadly. " I know. I am not a fool."

"We have shared everything for so long," said Lovell as he turned to Nicholai and held his face in his hands, "and we will always have those memories. But we must now act in an honourable way, for our own sake and Ellen's"

"Once you are married today, I will leave here and we will never see each other again. If that is what you want, it is the only way. But we must both agree."

"Yes. Our separation must be final. I couldn't bear it otherwise. Not even letters, do you agree?"

"Tempus omnia, semper amici!"

"That is not right. Time will not fly, but love will remain, my friend. Always the love will remain."

Chapter 8

Unfamiliar World
Christmas Eve – Randolph Hotel –
Oxford – Present Day

Everything was starting to become clear to me, dear reader. As I progress with my story I am starting to feel that you are my only true friend because you were not in any way responsible for my fate but, like me, an innocent and witness of the betrayal of those I imagined loved me as much as I loved them. How bitter my soul feels as I open my eyes to what is around me. How wretched it all seems whilst I am forced to witness the depravations and vileness of this present time, that I do not recognize as normal life. Better to have died in my rightful time and to have been oblivious of this one!

This December morning, in this hotel that feels bereft of the grace, elegance and charms it once wore so proudly, and ones I once witnessed in my lifetime, as a guest. It seems so different and devoid of any fine manners or deference of service, that back then would have been taken for granted.

As I make my way past the milling people, I slowly climb the grand turning staircase, so handsomely designed in its Victorian mock-gothic architecture, so popular when it was built in 1863. Many have suggested it resembles the Palace of Westminster in design, and it does. Indeed a famous parliamentarian by the name of Randolph Churchill, who called Blenheim Palace at Woodstock his home, was said to be the inspiration for the naming of this once grand, fine hotel. Perhaps those living in this strange present time consider it to be grand still, but it little compares to its atmosphere in my lifetime – as lost and haunted as I am in its current incarnation.

I silently climbed to the second floor, turning with the vast cantilevered stairs as they ascended. I wondered if this would be what it was like to climb to heaven and everlasting peace? Finally I made my way along the corridor, to Nicholai's suite of rooms and effortlessly passed through the door, to find myself standing at the foot of the bed. I was dazed and puzzled still, so crossed the room and looked from the window, unsure of why I had come here or what I had intended to do once arrived. My soul felt leaden and confused. The emptiness I felt seemed more acute than death.

Gazing from the window, I saw Charlotte arrive below in her horseless carriage and enter the hotel. The concierge, I now noticed, looked remarkably like the stable groom from Willow Manor, long ago; Rodgers I think his name was. He took her carriage and drove it into what had been the entrance to the hotel's stables. What would happen once she stood in this room I could not begin to guess. So I waited patiently for her to arrive.

For the first time, I began to feel anger and the need for revenge towards my sister, for her ill deeds in this life and the last, now so obvious to me – somehow I knew she was responsible for other things too, but it was still fully unclear as yet, although I now considered her deception and betrayal of me as unforgivable. That she tried to make my darling Lovell her own was too much to bear.

I could suddenly understand the power I was capable of exerting over her now, and she was oblivious of my abilities to harm her. Seeing her before me, I would choose to reveal myself to her, let her eyes see me, and watch them widen with horror and loathing at what stood before her. Then I would make her smell the stench of my decaying cadaver, intermingled with the fusted and rotted deterioration of my once exquisite wedding gown. Slowly I would clutch at her neck with my fleshless fingers, tightening the skeletal hands until her face turned slowly purple and blue as she struggled and gasped for air. I would savour every moment of her hideous and unbearable death and laugh, laugh, laugh into her mangled and contorted features. Her suffering in these final moments as but nothing compared to my own haunted existence for over one hundred years!

My vengeful thoughts were suddenly halted as I heard the bedroom door handle rattle as she unlocked the door and entered. I watched from the window and could see my reflection in the mirror opposite. In the last second I lost my nerve and allowed my reflection to dissolve away. Unseen again I observed.

She entered the room and, considering the violent confrontation between her, Nicholai and Lovell the previous evening in the Restaurant, looked remarkably calm and well groomed. Her face was seemingly free of any trace of strain or worry. That would not last for long, I thought, as I watched her cross towards the bed and stand at the foot – it took less than a second for her to register what she was seeing before her and to gasp in disbelief.

It took a few moments for Nicholai to sense someone was watching and open his eyes. As he did, this disturbed Lovell who was lying in his arms. Their comfort and attitude in this intimacy said more than words could.

"Christ, Charley!" said Nicholai startled to find her staring down at them. Her face was full of rage at what she was seeing. The pain at the betrayal she felt delighted me as I watched. I was glad. I laughed a giddy, shrill laugh, which echoed around the room but was audible to none but myself.

Lovell realized what was happening after a second or two. His first reaction was to try and get out of bed. "I'll go," he said to Nicholai, unable to look her in the eye.

Nicholai grabbed his arm and pulled him back into the bed. "No, I don't want you to go," he said with a determination whilst staring at Charley. "I can't run away from this anymore. It's over, Charley. I know what I want and it isn't you. I'm sorry."

If I'd had hands I would have clapped with delight. Charley's face was incandescent with suppressed rage. "Bastards!" she said with all the vitriol she could muster. With that she threw the room keys at them, turned on her heels and left, slamming the door as she went.

I watched as they collapsed back onto the pillows with visible relief on their faces. It then struck me that these two men had also betrayed me in that other life we had shared long ago. The fact that two men could share this kind of intimacy escaped me in life – it never occurred to me that such things even existed. Had what I witnessed, in fact, been a mirror image of what they had also done behind my back, prior to my wedding to Lovell?

The slamming of the door and the reverberation sucked me back to Willow Manor and before I knew it I was again in the attic as that sound of a crashing lid boomed and ricocheted through the manor. Bang, bang, bang, bang! The chest before me seemed to leap around the floor, as if someone inside tried to push open the lid from within. Then, as always before, the lid flew open and in the silence that followed I slowly walked forward, to peer inside at nothing but some remnants of the once silk lining of the linen chest.

Why did I keep having this terrible vision and nightmare? It was relevant to everything I was sure. But I had to find out why. Why was the chest always empty? Why did the house always draw me back to this? As I wandered back through the empty attic, the sound of my dress dragging along the floor was mingled with the sobs of my pain, at the realization that the man I had loved and waited for so long had betrayed me, in a way I little understood, prior even to my wedding. What an ignorant, foolish, stupid girl I had been. How could those I loved so much have done this to me – and also to each other? Love seemed an empty word to use now in the face of these revelations.

Today was Christmas Eve. As I wandered through my derelict home I could see glimpses of what had been long ago. The manor full of servants and the fires ablaze and the Christmas tree erected and lit in the grand stairway; the sound of carollers from the estate singing outside lustily, in the hope of a warm drink and a sweetmeat for their efforts. It all seemed like a dream when looking at the decay before me, the emptiness, the whispering of the wind creeping around me and mocking my loneliness. The mists rolled off the lake and crept slowly like some ravenous plague towards me, to swallow me up forever.

As I reached the top of the grand staircase, I heard voices. I waited as they grew nearer, but they were not instantly recognizable to me. Then I saw three people enter from the main front doors, the man among them pushing the unhinged great door a little wider, to allow easier access for the two women with him. They stood staring at the surroundings for a minute or so and they were speechless for some reason. I recognized them as the housekeeper, maid and concierge from the Randolph Hotel. It immediately struck me that they were the three I had seen at the hotel, who physically resembled staff I had known from the past: Florence, Millie and Rodgers the stable groom. Although they were not present reincarnations of those past lives in terms of recognizable spirits, their type had come here before with their chanting and mystic pretensions and hopes of speaking to the dead.

"This is so unfortunate," said Florence, "can you feel the sadness in this place? There is certainly a presence here, don't you think?"

"It is heart wrenching – the story or legend or whatever you call it," said Millie, "I have heard so much about this place and as much as I know I have never been here before..." she looked around and seemed lost for the right words, but then added, "but it is so familiar, like I know it intimately. How odd."

"It gives me the heebie-jeebies," said Rodgers. "If you want my opinion, there is something evil in this place. A great tragedy is absorbed in its fabric, or what's left of it. I am not sure we should interfere with whatever is going on here – or has gone on in the past." He then removed from his coat a huge bunch of mistletoe and handed each of them a sprig. "Hold onto this, it will help to protect you and demonstrate we only want to speak to the bride's ghost."

Watching them, my patience at their presence and conversation was fast waning. I found myself calling out to them softly, menacingly, and allowing them to hear it riding on the breeze that blew through the empty rooms.

"I'm here," I whispered, "what do you want from me? I am here, can you help me?"

I watched to see if any of them reacted and after a moment I saw Florence stiffen, then Millie. Rodgers looked at them puzzled.

"What?" he said anxiously, "What's the matter?"

"Did you hear that," said Florence raising her hand for silence, "did you hear that whispering, I heard it distinctly."

"I heard it too," said Millie, "she said 'I'm here' and 'help me' or at least I think someone did."

"I can't hear anything but the wind moaning and howling through the place, "said Rodgers. "It's your imaginations."

"It is Christmas Eve, it all happened on Christmas Eve in 1893, so the legend tells. Lady Ellen Forsyth had just married Lord Lovell in the family chapel."

At this revelation they suddenly had my attention. How did they know what had happened on my wedding day in 1893? I decided they would be of use to me, so I had to keep them here and find out more of what they had to say and why they had come here. Before me at the top of the stairs was a clump of old bottles, abandoned by some long forgotten tramp who had sought shelter in the empty manor. I focused my attention and made one of them start to slowly roll along the landing towards the top of the stairs.

The sound of this rolling bottle from the gallery above galvanized them and they huddled together, illuminated by the weak afternoon sunlight that suddenly burst through the gap in the front doors. I could see real fear in their eyes but also determination to face whatever was about to happen.

"There is someone else here," said Florence peering up into the gloom above, "keep calm and we will be okay. We don't mean her any harm."

"Maybe we should go," said Millie, "perhaps we shouldn't have come here – at least not today of all days."

"Do you really think it's her, Florence?" said Rodgers nervously. "Is it safe to have a séance, it could be dangerous. I said there was evil in this place…" He looked around and seemed the most uncomfortable of the group. "Don't forget we have to be back at the hotel for our shift tonight…"

The bottle reached the top of the stairs. It stopped and spun round a couple of times, glinting in the weak sunlight it caught their attention. They seemed to know I was in the manor, and also wanted to somehow get in touch with me. It brought to mind the tale Nicholai had told about séances and such things at dinner that evening long ago – how even Queen Victoria held them to talk to her departed Prince Albert. With that thought, I propelled the bottle off the top tread and allowed it to rattle and crash its way down what remained of the sweeping staircase until it smashed into a thousand pieces at their feet.

They stared at the remains of the bottle and then slowly looked up towards the gallery. I suddenly realized that Florence could see me. She said nothing to disturb the others. I turned and walked off towards the main bedroom corridor, towards where once my suite of rooms were. She watched me intently.

"Right, we need to go upstairs," she said to them. "Follow me and we will be okay." She crossed to the foot of the staircase, then turned back and indicated they follow her. "Just be careful of the treads as they may be rotten and your foot could go through."

They all slowly began to climb cautiously in pursuit of me and with high expectations of their forthcoming séance. Perhaps I would communicate with them and exceed their expectations of the spirit world – even let them all see the ghost of the Mistletoe Bride!

Back at the Randolph, Nicholai and Lovell had showered and dressed and were discussing their plans for the day. Nicholai had decided he wanted to visit Willow Manor again but this time he wanted to take Lovell with him.

"I just feel there is a reason why I must go back there," said Nicholai, to a less than convinced Lovell. "There is something about that place and there is a good chance we might find Charley there and try and make amends. I know she can be a bitch and she is not deserving of our pity but I don't want to part with bad feelings. If we talk with her, she will maybe start to understand and feel better about us."

"You really think so?" said Lovell, masking more than a little amusement in his voice, "after this morning's drama I feel it will take more than a little chat to smooth things over. I fear you are wasting your time…"

"Look, you are the one always telling me to face reality, be honest, be open about things. Well this is my way of doing that, so could I please have a little more support and less scepticism please?"

"I'm sorry – you're right. I just don't want you to be disappointed and only think it might be too soon to call a truce with Charley. She's hurting and angry and probably feeling a bit humiliated over it all – especially the way she found us this morning."

"That is why I need to do this – and why I need your help. It is also Christmas and I don't want to be a complete shit by ignoring her. Besides there is something weird about that manor I want you to see for yourself. It is odd, but I am sure I have been there before, and with you! How odd is that? Maybe I am just going mad, but indulge me and it will be a nice trip for the afternoon. Wait until you see the lake – it is so creepy!"

"I can't wait!" Lovell put his scarf round his neck and zipped up his coat. "Come on then, let's go and see this creepy place you have fallen in love with."

Lovell was finally coming back to Willow Manor, but all my hopes of his return were destroyed by the changed circumstances and the slowly revealed truth. How would I feel once he arrived here? Would Charley also arrive and allow Nicholai to agree an emotional resolution. Would any of them know that I was there and ready for their arrival?

Chapter 9

The Wedding Day
Willow Manor – Christmas Eve – 1893

A s dawn broke on the morning of my wedding to Lord Lovell, the servant's hall and kitchens were a buzz of activity. Most of us had decided to have breakfast in our rooms rather than have a formal affair in the dining room. It allowed for each of us to prepare for the ceremony, due to take place in the private family chapel in the early afternoon. The vicar from the parish church had agreed to conduct the ceremony – as he did most Sunday services for the family and staff at the manor, and we were used to his spirited sermons. Always uplifting.

Edward Miller, the said vicar, was a charming if not slightly eccentric character, who had the ability to make me laugh at the most inopportune moments, with his broad Lancashire accent that flattened all the vowels of his words. The effect was disarming, surprising and utterly ridiculous at times, and he was oblivious of the effect this had on me and others. Physically he was a fine man, with handsome features and striking dark curly hair. His blue eyes commanded attention and many of the female servants were affected by his presence; but less I suspect for his closeness to God or his reverence! Alas their feelings were in vain. His wife, for indeed he had one, was a little bird like creature who followed him dutifully and seemed always enraptured by him and ready to carry out any command he directed at her. They had several children already and a seventh Miller infant was well on the way. A most industrious couple indeed!

For myself the preparations that morning were calm and serene, to the point it worried me that I was not more agitated and nervous. Florence had taken the responsibility of being with me to help me with all the tasks at hand prior to the ceremony. We sat and had a leisurely breakfast in my small sitting room, adjoining my bedroom and bathroom. This was one of my favourite rooms as it contained many of my mother's personal pieces of furniture, all upholstered in shades of cream, with bright silk cushions in reds, dusky pinks and gold. It held her collection of brightly coloured pictures of Edwardian gardens in spring, summer, autumn and winter. There were two water-colours that depicted my mother in her youth and also after her marriage to Father. She always seemed so gentle and fragile in these paintings – as if she was fine china that would break so easily at a touch. Photographs, that new craze that replaced paintings, of my family also adorned various surfaces in their highly polished silver frames.

The curtains were festooned with beautiful roses, reflecting the colours in the cushions. The oil lamps were topped with crystal shades and highly polished brass bases. When a fire was lit in the small chimneypiece, as it was this morning, it was a cosy room that embraced one with a sense of well-being. In the window was a small side table, a clever invention that allowed it to be converted for taking tea or light meals, then flipped to become a handy card table with fine green baize. It also had useful secret compartments in which to store items of choice. That morning it allowed us to look out on the grounds, as we ate a modest breakfast that Andrews had kindly laid for us. He had also served tea in Mother's special silver service; such a thoughtful touch and one I appreciated very much indeed. Mother might not be with me on my wedding day in person, but these gestures ensured she was with me in another way – if not in spirit!

Because of Father's hatred of crowds and parties, the day would be quiet in terms of numbers. There was no great horde of guests arriving as one would normally expect at an aristocratic wedding. The time and date of year also made it inconvenient for most friends or acquaintances because of their own families and Christmas arrangements – not to mention the difficulties of traveling any great distances at this time of the year, with such unpredictable weather and conditions. It mattered not to me, dear reader, for you see, if I am honest, I also have an aversion to great crowds and it would have added to my anxiety and was also less to think about, or worry about anything that may have gone wrong. There would be a few local friends of Father's, estate workers, tenant farmers and house servants invited to celebrate later in the early evening. That was enough and well satisfied both Lovell and myself.

As I sat sipping tea that morning, I found myself thinking about the old ruins on the far side of the estate, close to the church, where the aforementioned Edward Miller was the vicar in residence, and the hamlet of Minster Lovell, where most of Willow Manor's workers lived in cottages belonging to Father's estate.

"Have you a favourite place on the estate, Florence?" I asked, taking her slightly by surprise. "A magical place perhaps?"

"The churchyard," she replied without a moment's hesitation, "at the edge of the village. You can see Willow Manor in the distance, through the ruins of the old medieval manor. On a spring morning, or winter evening, it is enchanting and always takes my breath away."

"Strange isn't it," I answered, without thinking why I thought it, "how Lovell's ancestor's once owned a manor on land that now belongs to Father's estate? It is like the land is coming back to him after several hundred years – strange how history sometimes repeats itself, isn't it Florence?"

"Maybe some things are just meant to be in this life. Lovell is a charming man and will make an exceptional husband and father." She looked at me and smiled and then blushed as she realized what she had said without realizing. "I am sorry, Ellen, forgive me. I didn't mean to be so personal, it just slipped out."

Her embarrassment amused me. "It is quite alright, Florence," I said quickly to ease her discomfort. "I hope too that Lovell will make a wonderful father someday – I also hope to make an equally wonderful mother and have lots of children. I always felt that Charlotte and I would have benefited from having other brothers and sisters – we would have been less insular and shy of society had that been the case, I am sure. A brother would also have been an heir for the title, so hopefully Lovell and I will make amends in that area. We have a duty to secure the future of Willow Manor and the baronetcy."

"Sometimes, Ellen," Florence said with real warmth in her voice, "I am delighted at how level headed you have become as a young woman. You have the best qualities of your late mother in that regard, of that I have no doubt. She was a fine, sensible and equally intelligent woman when it came to matters of duty and lineage and their importance for a family such as yours."

"Darling Florence," said I with a giggle, "I know my duty and what it is expected of me – an heir, and indeed a spare, will soon be anticipated by Father at the very least."

"You are correct of course," exclaimed a delighted Florence. "But marriage is also about many things apart from childbearing, Ellen."

"Thanks to your kindness and guidance, I am fully prepared for what is expected of me by my husband and the implications of one's wedding night especially! Although I am prepared in as much as, I have the knowledge but lack any experience, I am sure I will be happy to discover this side of married life with the help of my husband."

"Indeed. It is something that will probably fade with time and become less important in your marriage, that is when your relationship as friends and companions – and parents – will take precedence. Duty behind you, you will enjoy a fruitful life ahead with Lord Lovell. At least that is my dearest wish for you both."

"One thing that gives me the greatest pleasure of all, Florence, is that I shall remain living here with you, Father and Charlotte. As Lovell is without family and property, I shall not have to bear being carted off to some remote, draughty castle or manor to establish myself as the new mistress of the house, where the old retainers resent me and wish to make life hell! Imagine that, and I have heard tales of such horror from poor unsuspecting brides of the past."

"That is a blessing for us all, Ellen," she replied with much amusement and laughter. She then grabbed my hand and held it tightly. "I will always be here to watch out for you and to make sure your happiness is assured. You know that, don't you?"

I was struck by the sincerity of her tone and it made me feel suddenly emotional. My life would have been vastly different and undoubtedly less happy had Florence not been here to dedicate her life to Father and to us. We were all blessed to have her and I swore to myself I would make sure she was always looked after and cherished by us – for eternity for sure.

Florence then leapt up and was suddenly efficient again and ready to focus on the tasks to be completed if this day was to run smoothly. "Right, Ellen, I am going to run your bath. I will call you when it is ready. Finish your breakfast and relax a little in the meantime, it is the last opportunity you will have to do so!"

With that she left me to my own thoughts and I spent the time gazing out of the window and wondering what married life would feel like and if we would make a success of it. I smiled as I wondered what Lovell was thinking at this time and if he was also contemplating the future and what it held?

Dear reader – or should I now say, friend? Considering the intimacies I have thus far shared with you, as I recount this sorry tale that dammed me and my family, they are so personal that in life I would have only considered sharing them with someone who was a close friend or acquaintance. But then, when I now consider this, as I discuss the subject of friendships, I realize with a heavy heart that, in life, I had no such friend to which I could have confided. Neither did Charlotte, now I think on it with some concentration. We had both been schooled by Florence in later years, and a governess when we were in the nursery. Sad to say we never mixed with other children or young women of our age as we grew. Even on my wedding day, there were no friends to be bridesmaids, no maids of honour. This I fear was the fate of many women of our station in life, and perhaps Father was to blame for not encouraging us to mix with others of our class as children. It is not comfortable to dwell on what might have been. I cannot change what has been, no more than I can change what is yet to come. So, dear reader, I now consider you to be a friend because you have become intimately involved with me. From this point on it is how I will address you.

On that bright Christmas Eve morning, as the house prepared for the ceremony, I was fortunate to be secluded and serene in my preparations. Andrews had taken responsibility for seeing to my father's needs and acted also as his valet for that morning. This allowed for Father's valet and footman to act as thus for Lord Lovell and Count Romanov. Charlotte had volunteered to help our aunt with her needs before sorting out her own – which she was always happy to do. Charlotte hated fuss, and hated having any kind of help with bathing or dressing. It was only with sustained discussion and persuasion, and then with Father's insistence, she had agreed to act as my only bridesmaid. She openly declared to me that such a role would doom her to be an old maid forever! At the time this made me laugh as I thought she was only making a joke at her own expense. Fool I was to be so blind!

It may seem strange to say this to you, but the details of the wedding day seem somewhat confused and distant. I remember certain parts of the day clearly, but not others, it is like a cherished memory that one wishes one could retain in all its details and moments, but as the time moves on leaving the event in the past, everything becomes fogged and indistinct somehow.

If only a way could be found to preserve it in its full details, what a cherished possession that could be?

Florence arrived back in my rooms carrying my bridal bouquet, that had been made up by the estate gardener. It actually took my breath away when I first saw it. In spite of the plans and details I had agreed for its construction, the reality of seeing it far exceeded my expectations. It draped fully down in front of me as I held it, with a central core of the most beautiful white roses I had ever seen. They had been specially cultivated in the hot house and even managed to retain their powerful, sweet smell, so often lost when force grown out of season in that way. Interwoven between them and draping down was fresh mistletoe from the oak trees on the estate. Its distinctive leaves and white berries tumbled beautifully towards the floor. The variegated ivy punctuated the effect with a lush, dark green that made the whole almost vibrate with life. A matching headpiece was also made to attach my wedding veil. I could not have wished for better. As I looked at it, I knew that the family chapel would also be decorated to compliment this bouquet – it would be perfect for a Mistletoe Bride and her groom.

In her suite of rooms meanwhile, Charlotte was busily preparing her own plans for the day – most especially for events she was conspiring to create after the wedding and during the traditional game of hide and seek. She sat at her desk and looked from her sitting room window. She smoothed a piece of fine vellum writing paper and began to write a letter that would be delivered to Nicholai by pushing it beneath his door. She took a letter that had been written by Lovell so she could measure his hand and attempt to duplicate it. A convincing forgery was essential to her plans. If Nicholai suspected that it was not in Lovell's hand, he would surely ignore it and worse, alert Lovell to the fact that someone was conspiring against him. After several attempts in this moment, she was happy that she could convincingly write in his distinctive style. She had in fact practiced this fraud several times in recent days, to ensure she was accomplished. This is what she wrote:

Dearest Nicholai,

It is with great eagerness I write this letter to you on this my wedding day. In spite of my joy about this day, mingled with my feelings for you, I have always been honest and true in my regard to you and our relationship, however unconventional it has been. It is why I am so glad you are here to support me in my marriage to Ellen, however hard that is for you.

Please, Nicholai, grant me this one last request and meet me tonight, during the game of hide and seek, at the summerhouse down by the lake. There is something most urgent that I need to share with you. Please be discreet, and so shall I be. Tell no one and destroy this letter.

Until then. My love as always.

Lovell

Charlotte's face was contorted with disgust at the thought of their relationship – certainly one that would shock Father, and others, to the core. Her contempt for me was also rising to the surface as she put into motion a chain of events that would destroy every-thing – even for her. She wanted Lovell for herself but she was too blind to see that you cannot make another love you, if that love is not naturally there in their heart. Charlotte had always demanded everything of everyone. The more unpleasant side to her personality she reserved for the lower servants, who often felt her wrath.

Folding the forged letter and pressing her hand along the crease, she then slipped it into a matching cream vellum envelope. Picking up her pen she scribbled Nicholai's name across the front and underlined it – ensuring she copied Lovell's hand as she did. She then blotted the ink and slipped the envelope into her dress pocket, ready for delivery.

Gazing from the window and pleased that her plans were finally to be accomplished, she smiled and delightedly thought how, by the time the clock struck midnight, she would have succeeded in manipulating everything to suit her own desires. Suddenly she caught sight of Rodgers the groom, as he strode across the lawn below on his way to the stables. Sensing someone observing at him, he stopped and slowly turned to look up at the house. Seeing Charlotte looking out at him, he doffed his cap and smiled. He held her gaze for a moment and then buried his hands into his pockets against the cold as he strode off and disappeared behind a hedgerow. Charlotte smiled and remembered his rough handling. She had nothing but contempt for him and enjoyed toying with him to get him to do what she wanted. She touched the letter in her pocket and then laughed out loud at the irony of how the letter, Rodgers and Nicholai were interwoven as a result of her skilful manipulations. Rodgers would be waiting with his knife ready to slit the Russian pig's throat. How dare he force his attention onto Lovell, making him reject her so cruelly? It was Russian witchcraft and he deserved to die. It suited her plan for me, her sister, because, dear friend, my fate was also to be in the hands of her irrational and wicked mind!

My aunt was relishing the opportunity to relax and take her time with her toilet on this wedding morning. Indeed, by the time Millie had served her light breakfast of kippers, tea and toast with butter and fine English marmalade, it was nearly eleven o'clock! Still in her robe, she reclined on the sofa close to a roaring fire in the grate – also lit by Millie that morning before she then carried upstairs several pales of hot water for my aunt's bath. Thankfully, she had had the assistance of one of the footmen, so her efforts had been less strenuous than they would have otherwise been.

Charlotte had evidently allowed her charge for that morning to slip her mind, as she arrived to assist our aunt when most things were already completed. En-route she had taken a slight detour, being careful not to be seen by anyone, to Nicholai's suite of rooms. She had quickly looked right and left down the corridor and once she was certain she had not been observed, she took the forged letter from her dress pocket and bent down so she could slip it under the door. The task was not as easy as she had anticipated, the thick pile of the carpet on the hallway side made it rather difficult to get the letter under the door. She knew that on the other side there was a wooden floor, with a central Persian rug in the main room of the suite. Luckily this meant the letter could not accidentally slip beneath an inner carpet! Once her task was completed she stood up and hurried towards her aunt's suite.

She stood by the fire after kissing our aunt with a "good morning" greeting, then waited for Millie the maid to finish her task of collecting up the breakfast dishes and placing them on a tray.

"Can I serve you more tea, ma'am?" she asked whilst noticing Charlotte's impatience with her by rolling her eyes at the ceiling. Millie brushed her fingers over the scab above her eye – the result of the cut she sustained when Charlotte had pushed her aside in her rage, the day before, in the kitchens.

"No, thank you," replied my aunt. "I will ring when I need you to help me dress."

"That won't be necessary," said Charlotte. "I will help my aunt dress for the ceremony, so you won't be needed unless we ring for you."

"Yes, ma'am," replied Millie, with surprising cheeriness considering the dislike she had for Charlotte. "Thank you, ma'am," she said directly to my aunt, who in turn smiled at her warmly. Millie then lifted the heavy breakfast tray and carried it to the closed door. Charlotte crossed and opened the door for her to exit with a resigned, but highly audible, sigh of exasperation. She then shut the door on Millie's back.

"More tea, aunt?" asked Charlotte, as she poured herself a cup and added milk and sugar. "It's still nice and hot and a very good Indian tea."

"Thank you, Charlotte," she said as she passed her cup and saucer. "I have been so cold this morning, I wondered if I would ever get warm. That delightful maid, she has been so kind and helpful."

"You know my philosophy, aunt! Never fraternize with servants, it always leads to trouble. What is the saying? 'Familiarity breeds contempt'?"

"For goodness sake, Charlotte, you do talk such nonsense at times. I wonder where you get this hard, coldness in your personality. Certainly not from your father or mother! It must be a throwback to an earlier ancestor!"

"My dearest aunt, I am neither hard nor cold, just practical and realistic in the face of scheming servants and their whiles! You forget I have to run this house, and have for some years, indeed, since I was barely out of childhood, so I talk from bitter experience."

"Bitter indeed, Charlotte," said my aunt with an emphasis on the word 'bitter' that seemed to escape Charlotte completely. "I worry for you, Charlotte. You need to find yourself a husband and settle down. This life of a spinster is hardening you in a way I dislike."

"I would rather be a spinster than marry for convenience or money. Father has other plans for me, as you know dear aunt, and marriage is not one of them. My role is to run this mausoleum, tender to his needs, oversee the estate staff and the home farm workers. There is precious little time for anything else."

"I will speak to your father," said our aunt, "this is not right and if I can do one thing for you before I died, it is this!"

"Aunt, with respect, you forget one important thing," said Charlotte with real bitterness in her voice, "I am after all the plain one, am I not? Ellen is the beautiful, perfect sister with all the wit, grace and charms and soon she will also have the perfect husband in Lord Lovell. There is not much of anything left for me, is there?"

"Charlotte! I am feeling ever increasing concern because of such protestations," said our aunt, slightly shocked at the hurt in Charlotte's voice whilst she delivered this diatribe. "You also have rare talents and are, I have to insist, a fine looking young woman. You may not have conventional beauty, but you have a striking appearance that is just as attractive to the right man."

"Sadly, aunt, the right man is no longer available to me. He is otherwise spoken for."

"Now, there's an idea," said our aunt, "who could you be referring to?" She looked at Charlotte and then gasped as a thought entered her mind. "You don't mean Nicholai, surely?" She watched Charlotte for her reaction to this, but she turned to warm her hands in the fire. "I fear this may be an impossible subject for your affections, Charlotte, or indeed anyone else's."

"Nicholai?" said Charlotte with real anger and disbelief in her voice, "you cannot even consider I would have any interest in that Russian pig!" Her harsh words shocked our aunt into silence. She sipped her tea and tried to allow for a couple of moments reflection to enable Charlotte to calm herself. "I cannot stand that arrogant man and will be glad when he has gone from here for good. I only tolerate him for Lovell's sake."

In this instant my aunt suddenly understood that the man Charlotte coveted above all others was her soon to be brother-in-law, Lovell. She had had no idea up until this point in time that this was so, or of the implications it had for Lovell's future happiness and mine. She was also concerned at the obvious hatred she had discovered existed for Nicholai – it led my aunt to believe that Charlotte knew of the relationship between the two men and had somehow discovered this, probably by accident. Her guess was that Nicholai had rejected her and that, remembering the scene in the drawing room, where Charlotte and Lovell had been talking so intently, Lovell had also spurned her in her attempt to manipulate him by declaring her own feelings for him.

"Charlotte," said our aunt, "you must try and put this foolish anger behind you. If you allow things to blacken your heart, it affects your own happiness more than anyone else's. Please promise me you will seek out pleasant company and find friends of your own age. I will speak to your father – he is a selfish old man, as are many of us when years and infirmity cloud our judgment. Perhaps age makes us all selfish, but we need to understand that youth must have its day if it isn't to wither, turn sour and die prematurely."

"Forgive me, aunt," said Charlotte, realizing she had perhaps allowed too much emotion to spill out. "I am just nervous and tired after all the preparations for today's wedding. Of course I am a little jealous too!" She laughed brightly. "I am only human, aunt, and cannot help but wish it was me being married instead of Ellen. I mean no harm really." She helped our aunt rise to her feet from the sofa. "Please, we must start to get you dressed, otherwise we shall be late – and that dearest aunt is a prerogative only available to the bride today!"

"Don't be too harsh on your sister, Charlotte. She is so happy to be marrying Lovell and her face beams with delight whenever I look at her. It is an obvious love match and is not tainted by convenience or fiscal requirements. We should all celebrate that because so many young people from high families have no choice and little if any love in their marriage arrangements."

"Indeed so, aunt," said Charlotte as she then pulled the cord to summon the maid. "Now, you go to your bedroom and select your gown for the occasion and I will come presently to assist you with dressing."

"Thank you, dear. Please think deeply about what I have said and plan your means of escape. I am sure that other arrangements can be put in place to assist your father in his dotage. It doesn't mean you will be gone completely, just refocus your role in the running of this enormous house. You must, must have a life of your own, Charlotte and not be just shoulders on which a burden is placed."

With that my aunt retired to her adjoining room, little realizing that her kind, wise words were in fact lost on my sister. Her heart had already hardened and turned to the colour of ebony inside her chest. Her mind was now so poisoned by her own irrational rantings and assumed hurts and slights that anything our aunt said didn't even penetrate beyond the surface of her conscious, scheming mind.

A knock at the door alerted Charlotte that the maid had returned in response to her summons. After calling to her to enter, Millie appeared and moved towards her with some trepidation. "You called, ma'am?"

Charlotte wasted neither time nor words on her. "This fire needs attention. Bring up another scuttle of coal and see to it immediately. I don't want this room going cold and affecting Lady Marlborough's health." She turned and looked at Millie. "Well? Get on with it girl!"

Millie poked the ashes through the grate, then picked up the coalscuttle and emptied the remains of the contents onto the fire. She then slid the draft panel open to create a good draw. Standing, she picked up the heavy scuttle and made her way from the room to start the not inconsiderable journey to the basement, to fill the scuttle as instructed. As she left she bobbed a slight curtsey to Charlotte, who remained unresponsive and impassive as usual. Once Millie had left the room, Charlotte feigned a bright smile and joined her aunt in the bedroom to help her dress.

Down in the family chapel, Andrews, in-between making sure

Father was dressed and ready, was also making sure the decorations were all in place. The small altar and two large church candleholders of silver, standing well over six feet in height, were all decorated with the same cream roses, ivy and mistletoe as adorned my headdress and bouquet. The aisle end of every pew was also similarly adorned with a small decoration made of the same. The smell of heavily scented incense managed to mask the smell of dampness that always pervaded the chapel, especially during the winter months. There were also oils of Frankincense and Myrrh in small candle burners dotted here and there – these gave a lovely warm aroma that was both relaxing and heightened the senses pleasurably for a winter wedding.

Since their conversation at sunrise, Lovell and Nicholai had not met again and didn't intend to until they would make their way to the chapel, after lunch, for the ceremony. They had spent their time getting ready with a valet (actually two footmen who took that role for the day) in their private rooms. Their thoughts were their own and they communicated with nobody else that I was aware of. Nicholai had found Lovell's letter pushed under his door and after seeing his handwriting on the envelope had not been able to open and read it – instead he put it in the inside pocket of his naval dress uniform jacket that he had decided to wear for his best man duties. It surprised him to get the letter because they had agreed that there would be no more discussion or communication, even by letter, after their decision this morning. Nicholai just wanted this duty to be over so he could leave this place as soon as he could. He had already asked Andrews to organize a coach and four to take him to Oxford, after the wedding and the main festivities were over. That way he could slip away at an appropriate moment unseen and unhindered. He patted the letter in his pocket and thought perhaps it should go on the fire unread. Instead he opened it and read the contents, whilst pouring himself a large drink of vodka from his own flask. The letter puzzled him, as it seemed to go against everything that they had said and agreed that morning in Lovell's bedroom. Nicholai folded the letter and put it back in his pocket. Perhaps he should go to the summer house and meet Lovell for one last time – if he decided not to go, it would seem a good time for him to slip away during the game of 'hide and seek'. It seemed an odd thing to do at a wedding, but he never underestimated the English when it came to strange and eccentric customs!

My own preparations were nearing completion. Florence had helped me dress in my fine, cream silk wedding gown, with a full skirt that rippled and flowed with every movement. I could now see why the dressmaker required all those alterations and adjustments. It was perfection to behold – at least to me, as I looked at my reflection in the full-length mirror. It also felt extraordinary to wear, fitting me in such a way as to be completely comfortable and effortless to move about in. Gazing in that mirror, looking at the intricate mistletoe embroidery, created with fine cream, green and golden silk threads was enchanting. The intricate beading work on the bodice, with small diamonds placed to represent dew drops on the embroidered roses thereon, brought a tear to my eye. The whole was so beautiful and yet its purpose was so fleeting. In a few short hours I would be married and the usefulness of the dress would be at an end. How extraordinary to think such a thing at such a time as this. There was something of the melancholy about it. As I looked at the reflection, it seemed somehow unreal, as if it were all just an illusion; a dream that I would wake from and never be able to recover.

My mind and imagination was working overtime and my face went suddenly ashen. Florence put her arm round me and I could see the concern in her eyes.

"What is the matter, Ellen?" she asked, "do you feel unwell? Is something wrong?"

"I don't know," is all I could initially say coherently. "I feel somehow strange and light headed and the reflection I saw in the glass was..."

"Was what, Ellen?" She steadied me with her arm and I began to feel better just because her presence made me feel safe. "Do you want to sit down? Can I get you some water perhaps?" she asked me with increasing concern.

"No, no, I will be fine. I don't want to crease the dress by sitting down. That would be a sin after all the hands that have toiled on it for me."

"What reflection did you see in the glass, child?" Florence must have been truly worried at that moment as she never called me "child" anymore unless she feared for my health or well-being.

"My reflection was confused, it made no sense," I said, still bemused and a little disorientated. "I seemed as I am now but the room around me was empty and derelict beyond my recognition. It seemed I was in another room somewhere else...I then seemed to change also..."

"You are nervous and a little overcome with the emotion of the day, Ellen. It is your mind playing tricks I believe, that is all child."

"I seemed to age in the mirror, my dress seemed to wither and decay before my eyes, and all in an instant, before I appeared normal again. Worse, my face took on the image of an old woman...then a skull, Florence. Do you think it is an ill omen of some kind?"

"You, young lady, have an overactive imagination! Old woman indeed." She looked into the mirror with me and smiled. "See at how beautiful you are Ellen, how wonderful you look on your wedding day and how proud Lovell will be when you join him at the altar soon; a picture of health and hope for the future."

Little did I realize it then, dear reader and friend, but in that instant I had indeed seen the future, a future that flashed before me in the last minutes before my wedding as if warning me to something. I wish I could have taken heed of that warning but alas I was ignorant and blind to it all. Even had I known and could have seen ahead and what fate had in store for me, I could have done nothing. It was meant to be and nothing could now alter the inevitable. Charlotte's plans had also started to roll onward towards their conclusion. I was doomed, along with everyone else.

The rest is a blur – I was in a daze. I recall walking down the grand staircase on the way to the chapel on Father's arm. It all seemed to be in slow motion when I remember it now – a lamb that was me, led to the slaughter. The staff stood in the hallway smiling, some crying and drying their eyes, some gently applauding and gasping as they admired my bridal gown. All the while, Father was beaming his best smile – even his eyes seemed to shine brightly and were full of love and hope.

We entered the chapel and they all seemed overcome by the occasion. I felt numb, as if I didn't really belong there, as if it was all a mistake. The faces of Charlotte, Florence, Father and my aunt all seemed hideous and distorted into grimaces that frightened me. Nicholai looked stern and uncompromising and Lovell turned and seemed worried. The vicar was smiling and waiting at the altar, his wren-like wife played the foot pump organ. She smiled whilst working the pedals of the organ with her feet to make sure enough wind supported the melody as I walked down the aisle. Father handed my arm to Lovell and we turned and faced the vicar. His mouth moved and I knew what was happening but it made no sense. I do recall he got to the point when he asked if anyone had any reason why this marriage could not proceed. In the few seconds silence that followed I now wonder what was going through the minds of those with secrets and lies hidden from view. There were just impediments aplenty!

Chapter 10

Destiny
Willow Manor – Oxford – Present & Past

It was not an ill-wind that blew through the ruins of Willow Manor this cold Christmas Eve afternoon, but a wind of resolution and change. Coldness like warmth was alien to me now as I had no sense of either, as do those with living flesh. It did not occur to me to consider that any kind of change was blowing my way after so many years of being trapped in spirit, as my home decayed and then was abandoned until I was left alone.

As I wandered the vast empty attic spaces and listened as the wind moaned and whistled its way through every nook and cranny, I felt compelled to keep coming back time and again to the same spot. As I approached this familiar place, I could see ahead of me the old linen chest, with the remains of its pink, silk lining tattered and decayed into remnants that clung on determinedly – it reminded me of my own situation as I hung on with skeletal fingers, for what seemed now a lost hope or dream. Fantasy would perhaps be a better descriptive. But for what, I wondered? Did I even know anymore? Even if Lovell did return, I wondered if I would even know him anymore – or indeed any of them that I had known in life? To say my mind was in turmoil and confusion would be to understate my situation.

As I looked from the attic window, across the expanse of the grounds to the lake beyond, in the weak wintry sunshine I could see the mists start to roll across the lake like a huge, swirling armada of phantoms, steadily creeping their way towards the manor – engulfing the old summerhouse. In that moment I felt there was something quite beautiful about the mists and that they were not in the least frightening – they often unnerved people and I could never understand why that was so.

The wittering of voices in the far off distance only gradually caught my attention. At first they were so indistinct I considered them to be nothing but the wind as it blew in, around and down the hundreds of chimneys, or miles of corridors and empty window casements at Willow Manor. Then it became clearer as the wind's direction changed and carried the words to me as it whined through the empty house.

The mistletoe hung in the manor hall
The holly branch shone on the old oak wall
The Baron's retainers were blithe and gay
Keeping the Christmas holiday...

The strange voices were not singing the lyrics as you would with a song; they seemed to chant them in unison, as if trying to emphasize every word. The words seemed somehow to reflect the manor in my father's time and it suddenly occurred to me it might be the three people I had seen earlier, who resembled the staff of 1893. By thought I was in my old suite of rooms and I listened intently as they chanted again. I didn't understand at first what the meaning was, but it soon became apparent to me as I listened:

The Baron beheld with a father's pride
His beautiful child, Lord Lovell's bride.
And she with her bright eyes seemed to be
The star of the goodly company.

Oh, the mistletoe bride!
Oh, the mistletoe bough!

They were seated at a makeshift table, jumbled together from some bits of old wood and furniture, in what had once been my cosy sitting room that in life I had derived so much pleasure from and where I had prepared for my wedding all those years ago – a wedding these people were now relaying back to me in this strange verse.

"She's here," said the one who looked like Florence, "I can sense her, feel her in the room with us."

"Will she talk to us," said Millie, "or is she not aware of us?"

"I'm going to light a fire in that grate – I am freezing," said Rodgers, "I can't concentrate I am so bloody cold!"

"Hush," said Florence, "you will scare her away. Light the fire but be quick about it, we don't want to lose the connection."

I watched transfixed as he hurriedly screwed up some old newspapers, found scattered on the dusty, bare floor. He then broke some bits of wood that had once been chair legs and placed them on the paper. Taking out a box of matches, he fumbled to light a match – his trembling hands were so cold it seemed to make his task impossible. Finally he managed to strike one and it flared into flame as he lit the newspaper and the chimney, so long dormant, quickly drew the air and caught the flames that began leaping up and out of sight. The room was suddenly awash with flickering light and the three faces were illuminated, aiding the impossible job of the weak daylight fighting to pierce the dust-laden and grimy windows and embrace the room within.

"Hurry now, Rodgers," said Florence. "We must concentrate and hope she will trust us and be able to communicate with us. Today is a special day for her, she may be at her most receptive to us because of that"

"Do you think she will know who we are?" asked Millie. "After all, she may think we are nothing but strangers invading her home?"

Suddenly, and for no apparent reason, Millie burst into tears and could not stem the flow as she sat touching hands with the others.

"I'm so sorry, but it was her wedding day and it was all so sad for her." She sniffed and snuffed and then pulled out a hanky and blew her nose so hard it echoed through the vastness of the manor and brought them all to silence. "Lady Ellen needs to know who we are, Florence. I think it may be important and make a difference to her."

It made me focus my attention and help them along in the hope they would reveal more. I crossed and stood behind Florence and gently I placed my fleshless fingers on her neck, and then withdrew them slowly to allow for a greater impact. She shuddered at my touch and began to shake violently – it took her a few moments to regain her composure.

"She's here, I felt her, and she means us no harm I am sure." She then began to speak to me with a firm, confident voice. "Lady Ellen, we are here to help you and wish you no ill. We are all familiar with your life and the tragic end you suffered on the day of your wedding to Lord Lovell." She seemed to pause, to see if I was there and had heard this information. I obliged by making the door swing closed with a jolt and a bang. This seemed to satisfy them, going off the shriek Millie ejaculated, that made them all jump in spite of themselves. "We three are all descended from family members who worked at the manor in your lifetime. They were servants here."

This last piece of information helped me to understand why they all looked so familiar to me – and I then realized, they had inherited their ancestor's physical characteristics that made them so familiar to look at.

"Let's try the chant again," said Rodgers, "it may help to keep the connection open."

"Let's do the next section, it may help her to remember that day and what was happening," said Millie.

"No," said Florence, "we'll repeat the second verse again. We need to be sure."

Florence nodded an instruction and then they again touched

hands and concentrated expressions veiled their collective faces.

The Baron beheld with a father's pride
His beautiful child, Lord Lovell's bride.
And she with her bright eyes seemed to be
The star of the goodly company.

Oh, the mistletoe bride!
Oh, the mistletoe bough

These words swept me back to that day in 1893 and reminded me of my happiness and delight at having at last married my darling Lovell. After the ceremony, the first thing Father insisted on was unveiling the portrait in the main drawing room. We all gathered and he finally allowed the silken cloth to be shed from the work of art he had so proudly commissioned. It was also the first time that dear Lovell had ever been allowed a viewing, lest it be bad luck for me. It was immediately apparent that the commission had been an unusual one and explained the reason the drawing room had been out of bounds for so many weeks prior to this wedding, during the previous summer.

Father, in his youth, and not unusual for his station, had taken the grand tour of the continent prior to going up to Oxford. Whilst there, he had explained to us all, he had been impressed by the beauty and permanence of the art of fresco paintings. This, he described briefly to us, involved creating a painting that was literally painted onto wet plaster that then dried. Layer upon layer was built up to add depth and character. It was a complex, time consuming and difficult operation but he felt it was appropriate for this gift, as it would have permanence and would be safer from damage than a conventional portrait on canvas. No doubt it was also very expensive but that was never mentioned. The fresco itself was bordered with a conventional gilt frame, to make it fit in with the other family portraits surrounding the walls, but of course this could be removed without harming the fresco portrait itself.

As we all gazed at the portrait and took this information in, I was immediately struck by the details and lifelike image of myself, enlarged for eternity and literally embedded into the walls and plaster of Willow Manor. The detail on the fine string of pearls was exquisite and it seemed that some perpetual light caught them individually and gave them real depth and reality. Beneath the whole, on the gilt frame, was a small brass plaque that recorded the details: 'Lady Ellen Forsyth on the occasion of her marriage to Lord Lovell. December 24th, 1893. A Mistletoe Bride.' No daughter could ever have been paid a more touching and lasting tribute by her father. I was overwhelmed and humbled.

The wedding breakfast was held in the ballroom and we all enjoyed a light lunch of cold meats, salads and the usual delicacies associated with Christmas time. We did not want a formal, many coursed meal, because it would have been too much food to allow for any dancing and other games, that would naturally follow the afternoon's celebrations. My memory of all this past gaiety is now sparse and time has allowed many details to diminish or vanish altogether. I do know and remember that my spirit was as light as air and it seemed that all of life and my future years were spread before me. If ever I was truly happy, it would have been in those few hours.

Once lunch was over, some retired to refresh themselves and have a short rest before the dancing began. Father had hired several musicians, to create a small orchestra for dancing his favourite waltzes. I remember laughing at the time and thinking how fortunate it was that a waltz was also my chosen dance of pleasure; especially in Lovell's embrace, as it was truly like floating on air when I was in his arms.

"Lady Ellen," said Florence breaking me from my thoughts, "are you still with us?

It took me a moment to orientate myself as I forgot where I was and the realization dragged me back to reality and the present. I looked at the three expectant faces sitting before me and couldn't help but see the tragedy that was my current situation. I had seen these kinds of people in the past coming to the house, holding hands and desperate to contact me or any other lost spirit that they imagined roamed the place. It was just me and usually I had no time for such foolishness. However, I was drawn to these people because I had made a connection – their ancestors had been alive in my time and I knew them.

Rodgers rose and crossed to the fire and tried to poke the ashes with a piece of wood he found discarded in a corner. He then broke some more wood, remnants of old furniture, mostly rotten and full of woodworm, he had spied in a corner. I wondered if these were relics of my dear mother's furniture that I had once cherished and loved in this very room? The thought was too painful so I dismissed it and watched as they reconvened around the table now he had added wood fuel to the fire. It roared gently as the draft caught it and made the embers glow red hot, as it was carried up the chimney. Just as they were to start their chant again, I heard another voice, far off, probably outside, call out. The stillness was palpable as everyone froze and decided if they had heard it or imagined it.

Lovell and Nicholai had pushed through the service gate in the boundary wall to enter the grounds. Nicholai had remembered it from that first day he had come here with Charley. They walked along the gravel drive and turned the corner to approach the house. Here they stopped and took in the view. Lovell was silent and felt moved nearly to tears, a reaction that surprised him immensely.

"Hello," called Nicholai. "Hello?"

"Do you think she got your text message, Nicholai?" asked Lovell, still staring at the derelict manor. "I haven't seen her car anywhere."

"Don't worry, she'll be here. She wouldn't miss an opportunity for some kind of revenge, that's for sure."

"Sometimes, Nicholai, you can be a heartless bastard. She didn't ask to be involved in this mess – don't forget we created the mess in the first place and you made it worse by thinking you could play in two lives at once! Idiot!"

"Hey, don't give me such a hard time. I'm doing my best to sort this out and do the decent thing. It's why I want to talk this through. Maybe we can even remain friends in the long run."

"I wouldn't bank on that if I were you."

"Hello?" shouted Nicholai again. He then looked and saw the chimney. "Lovell, look at that," he said pointing up to the roof." Can you see the smoke coming from that stack; it means someone has lit a fire inside the manor somewhere. Come on then, what are you waiting for?"

They strode towards the house, intent on finding Charley and to see if she was responsible for the smoking chimney. Instead of entering they carried on past the old stables, to the front view of the manor, overlooking the lake. Their intention was to look up at the windows, to see if any glimmer of light would give away the location of the room in which the fire was lit.

I had decided that the messages they could send each other, via their handheld little machines, like telephones, were in fact similar to what in my day would have been a telegram or post card. They seemed similarly short and to the point. The only difference being they arrived on the machines and a noise would be heard to indicate their arrival. They also used these for speaking as Father would have done on his telephone – newly installed at the manor, with great excitement, I now remember, in the summer of 1892 – but it was hardly used and rarely rang at all – if it ever did, it always seemed to as Florence or Andrews happened to be passing and they would nearly jump out of their skin at the shrill ringing sound! It was infrequent, I suppose, because not many people had them at that time. Their existence was more novelty than practicality back then; only rich aristo-crats and merchants available to afford them. They had no wires that I could see, so is it any wonder I considered them some kind of spiritualist's or medium's devices, as I had no knowledge or understanding of how they worked.

Unbeknown to Lovell and Nicholai, Charley had received the message and was indeed on route to Willow Manor. The reason for her visit was far removed from theirs. She was determined to see the conversion of our home and wanted to concentrate on work and think less about the mess her relationship was in with both Nicholai and Lovell. She was currently driving her horseless carriage through Oxford.

The fact that Lovell was finally back in my world excited me more than I ever imagined it could. His arrival at Willow Manor had been anticipated for so long and now the day had arrived it seemed almost to be an anti-climax. Nothing really changed and I began to feel that my hope would be instrumental in setting me free from this terrible entrapment. I had placed so much faith in him, that he would be able to set me free and that our love would continue from whence it was so quickly cut short all those years ago. That was now a dream in tatters.

I watched from the window and could see them crossing what had once been neatly manicured lawns, but what now resembled a withered, winter meadow of long grasses. Beyond was the lake and the old summerhouse, encircled as it usually was with the rolling mists. They looked so determined and so at ease with one another. It was for some reason quite hard to watch them, as it made me feel rather detached and rejected. It was then I remem-bered it was Christmas Eve afternoon and around the time we had enjoyed our wedding service in the chapel. By thought alone I found myself standing where the altar once stood. Where we had exchanged our vows amidst smiling, happy faces.

Looking up at the stained glass windows in their perfect gothic arches of sandstone, some boarded over long ago, I could see the destruction and decay and hear the chill wind and remnants of mist creeping through into this now hostile place that had no comfort or warmth. The floor was littered with rotted wood and decaying leaves. Old rubbish gathered in the corners and the ceiling was nothing but laths without their clinging plaster, huge holes were punched into them and the room above could be seen with ease; great beams of weak sun, with dust particles dancing in the wind, frantically swirled within them. The wind began to whistle with a menacing tone, so I felt the need to get away from there. Whatever joy and reverence this room had once witnessed was long gone – nothing remained but the desolation it had also rendered my memories.

I rushed from that place because I could no longer bear the weight of loss on my weary soul. I felt trapped, as if unable to breathe and didn't know why that should be. I had long since left behind the necessity to fill my lungs with air. That ended once my life did. I found myself carried by the mist and the wind towards the summerhouse and the lake beyond began to beckon me to it. I hated water in life and still retained the fear of it in death. I could hear the whispers of the water calling to me. "Come to me, Ellen," it would request over and over again until I felt I would scream. I would rush as fast as I could in another direction, just to get away from it. Why did it call me so, dear reader and friend, why?

Nicholai and Lovell were standing near the summerhouse and gazing back at the manor, still trying to trace the room, or at least its vicinity, in the hope they would find it easier once they entered.

"She's on her way," said Nicholai as he looked at the text message. "I guess we'll have our chance with Charley."

"Is she coming out to meet us?" said Lovell, still staring at the manor and the lone curling swirl of smoke rising from a chimneystack. "She wants to be careful she doesn't set the place on fire."

"What?" said Nicholai. He then realized what Lovell meant. "No, she's not here yet, she's driving through Oxford and will be here in about half an hour or so, depending on traffic."

"But if she isn't in there lighting a fire – who is?"

"I guess we should go in and find out. Probably a vagrant or drug dealers."

"I'm not sure if that is such a good idea – it could be dangerous."

I then realized they had no idea about Florence, Millie and Rodgers, who were holding their séance in the manor in my old sitting room. So obsessed had I been with Lovell's arrival, I had quite forgotten about them, until this conversation brought them back into focus. At that moment the door of the summerhouse began to bang loudly as the wind tried to close it against its will.

The noise of the banging jolted Lovell and Nicholai and seemed to unnerve them. Suddenly, and against my will, I was dragged back to the deserted attic and then I knew what was going to happen. Once again I was subjected to that terrible nightmarish experience. Before me the trunk seemed to jolt and rattle on the floor, as the sound of the lid slamming shut reverberated through the manor – its volume seemed increased greatly and it ended as quickly as it started. But this time the lid remained shut tight. I crept forward and could see a sprig of mistletoe crushed where the lid met the body of the chest. After a moment I could hear scratching and scraping from within. It increased in volume and became frantic, then, just as suddenly, stopped. I could hear a sobbing woman, someone very distressed and unhappy. It took a few moments for me to realize the sobbing was my own.

Florence was doing her best to calm Millie and Rodgers, as the noise of the slamming chest lid echoed through the empty manor. They also heard my pitiful sobbing. The colour drained slowly from their faces as the implications of this event began to register.

"She is here," said Millie. "She must be here, it can't be anyone else. Can we help her to be free of this, Florence? Can we?"

"Quiet, girl!" said Florence sharply, "we need to keep our concentration and not let our reactions spoil the connection we have been lucky to make. We need to invoke the spirits of the past to try and release her."

"That noise, what was it?" asked Rodgers with a whisper. "It seemed to shake the house but it came from above, I think."

"Probably the attic," said Florence. "That is where it happened I understand."

"I can't bear to think of it. Shall we try the next verse?"

"It can't do anything but help, Rodgers, so we may as well. I have a feeling that fate is with us today – perhaps the anniversary of the event has added clarity to the connection we have made with her spirit. I am sure it is her."

Strength in silence I thought. With that in mind I watched transfixed as Florence began to concentrate her mind on the task at hand. There would be no other spirits here to enthral them apart from mine. As I watched, her face began to change and contort as if it were suddenly transformed into hot, dripping wax. Her features began to melt away.

"She's changing, Rodgers, she does this when she connects. It's why she's called a trans-medium."

"Shit! I really don't like this, why doesn't she say anything?"

"Quiet and don't be an idiot. It will disrupt her and it could be dangerous."

"I knew I shouldn't have come here. I should have known that it was a bad idea when you told me about this place at the hotel. My great-great-grandfather may have worked here along with your ancestors, but that doesn't give us the right to interfere in things we don't understand."

I watched as Florence's face seemed to contort and twist into odd, indiscernible shapes. I was drawn to her and crossed to stand behind her. As I watched the back of her head and the distressed faces of Millie and Rodgers, my face was suddenly plunged forward by a force I did not recognize, until it was pushed through her skull and her face took on the appearance of my own. This quickly changed to my living flesh features and I could once again feel the sensation of breathing and having a heart beating in my chest, although I realized it was Florence's. It was almost too painful and brought with it a surge of regret for lost life.

"It's her," said Millie, as she stared at my youthful face, still looking directly at her. "Keep still, Rodgers, you may frighten her away."

"What do you want from me," I said, with a hint of anger in my voice. "Please leave this place, my home, you have no right to interfere." It only then occurred to me that Florence was speaking with my voice.

"Where is Florence?" asked Rodgers becoming more and more agitated. What happened to her voice for God's sake? I can't stand this anymore…"

"Shut up and keep still!" I shrieked at him, with so much force it made their hair almost stand on end. "You want to leave this place do you? I have wanted to leave for an eternity compared to you but I am stuck here in this desolate, empty tomb!"

Rodgers and Millie were frozen in fear and just stared at me for the longest few seconds.

"We just wanted to help you, Lady Ellen," said Millie, "to help you be free of this place and move on – to give you peace at last. It is only because we know of your plight that we came to help you."

"Yes," said Rodgers a little nervously at first, "we were talking at work – we all work at the Randolph Hotel…"

"I know where you all work," I said, "I have seen you there too in recent days."

"We were chatting about our families and we realized we all

had ancestors who had worked at Willow Manor and knew the story of your wedding, as it had been passed down. Our families all still live near Minster Lovell…it's why we came here today to help…"

I had had enough and stood back from Florence and began to observe them all again from outside her.

"She's gone," said Millie, "Florence's face is changing again."

"Is Florence coming back? Is she, Millie?"

As I watched, Florence's face began to take the shape of a face I never imagined I would see again. Slowly my mother's features began to appear and she seemed to be searching the room looking for me.

"Ellen, you must go to the lake," she said. "You must go to the lake!"

"Who is it," said Rodgers, "Who is she talking to?"

"I'm not sure who she is but she is talking to Lady Ellen, not us. She wants her to go to the lake."

"Why?"

"I don't understand. Perhaps she has to meet someone there? I honestly don't know.

"Please, Ellen, listen to me as it's very important that you do not listen to Lovell or Nicholai. Do you hear me, Ellen? Go to the lake, darling, to the lake."

With that my mother's face disappeared and Florence's began to transform again into her own. Her whole body began to shake and her eyes suddenly flashed open. They stared into the room and sought something or someone they could not see. The beads of sweat trickled down her face and the shaking slowly subsided.

"Chant the next verse," said Florence's weak voice at last. "Chant the next verse quickly. We must keep the connection going."

Millie and Rodgers looked at each other with trepidation but silently decided to chant the next verse as instructed by Florence.

Oh the mistletoe bough!
Oh the mistletoe bride!

'I'm weary of dancing now,' she cried;
'Here tarry a moment, I'll hide, I'll hide,
'And Lovell be sure you are the first to trace,
The clue to my secret hiding place.'

Oh the mistletoe bough!
Of the mistletoe bride!

Away she ran, and her friends began
Each wing to search and each nook to scan
And young Lovell cried, 'Oh where do you hide?
I'm lonesome without you, my own fair bride.'

Oh the mistletoe bough!
Oh the mistletoe bride!

The sheer joy and excitement of my wedding day was yet to be punctuated with dancing, in the ballroom, after high tea, then the most exciting and traditional part would be the game of hide and seek. I know reader and friend you may see this as something rather odd and eccentric but it was a traditional thing to do at the wedding of a mistletoe bride. Perhaps, I often thought, it was a way to allow the bride and groom some private moments, to steal an embrace or a kiss prior to the wedding night, amidst the revelry of the day! That at least was my secret hope of the event!

My father was determined to have a small orchestra for the evening so that he could enjoy a waltz or two with me, Charlotte and perhaps even our aunt – although Lady Marlborough (as she was always addressed in company) never danced in the presence of anyone – if she ever did at all! It always surprised me somewhat, as in other respects she was a woman before her time and rarely stayed by outdated traditions or social requirements or expectations. Conundrum was the word best used to describe her.

To see the chandeliers blazing with their new candles for the occasion was something to behold and so rare an occasion that many had never seen the room opened for such gaiety, let alone sighted the magnificence of the two, huge, drop crystal chandeliers. The art of lighting the near one hundred and fifty candles on each of them was almost a military operation. There were two concealed winches that Andrews would wind to slowly lower them, so that the footmen could reach the candles on foot or by ladder, to successfully light them with handheld, thick tapers. Once lit, they would be wound up by the winch and thus illuminate the ballroom, along with the numerous wall sconces holding half a dozen candles each, decorating the huge mirrors that adorned the walls, along with paintings and further family portraits. As the said candles were specially made to be slow, bright burners, there was no fear they would not last the evening well. One can imagine the brilliance and beauty they created in the magical room. The two, huge, marble fireplaces at each end of the ballroom were lit and loaded with roaring logs to give warmth; after all it was a cold winter evening and the need of fires throughout the house had managed to create a cosy, warming atmosphere, except in the further reaches of the manor, where the icy grip of winter was still able to clutch at your ankles, should you venture there!

As Father and I, watched by a beaming Lovell, danced to a Strauss waltz and found ourselves carried away by the music and the moment, Charlotte was in conversation with Nicholai, on the far side of the ballroom. Their conversation at the time I had no idea of, but now, dear reader and friend, as I relay this to you, I can tell you its content, although it may or may not shock you, depending on your opinion of my sister thus far.

David Slattery-Christy

"Nicholai," she said with warmth, "could I bother you for a few moments? You must admit that although you obviously loathe me, and I must add the feeling is quite mutual, you will realize that it would look somewhat odd in the present company on this occasion, not to at least exchange what seems to be pleasant conversation – however trivial." She looked him straight in the eye, with her own cold ones glinting delightedly."

"Charlotte, you underestimate and misunderstand me completely," he said with equal aloofness but resigned indifference to her games. "My admiration for your father, and beautiful sister, command me to respect them in this, their home. The disregard I feel for you is forgotten and demands no attention of my private thoughts. Nor ever will again after this day."

"Indeed, sir," said Charlotte with forced gaiety and a little laugh to allude to civility between them should anyone be watching. "It is a shame that your private thoughts could not also discard the lustful feelings you have, and enjoy physically, from what I witnessed since you have been a guest here, for my new brother-in-law? Very Oscar Wilde! I am sure my sister would be delighted to hear such news on this of all days?

"My dear Charlotte," said an obviously concerned Nicholai, "should you even begin to think about suggesting and voicing such slander to your sister or anyone else, I will gladly enjoy breaking your neck with my own hands. Do I make myself clear?"

"Oh, dear, Nicholai. You disappoint me. I thought you would have more about you than issuing mere threats – one's that you would never be able to carry out. After all, I would have no choice but to tell my father that your seed is growing within?" Charlotte patted her stomach gently and smiled horrifically in his face.

"That is a lie and absurd!"

"Of course it is, but will be believed by Father should I tell

179

him. I couldn't possibly admit to being pregnant by a stable groom – although at least he could satisfy me and didn't wither away in the moment and become incapable as did you, sir."

"I will deny this, and denounce you as a liar and a cheat."

"Do as you must, darling Nicholai. The die is cast, soon you will be exposed of dishonouring me and Father will insist you marry me. After all, now I will have no prospect of having any other husband – a spinster with an illegitimate child will make me a social outcast." She looked at his face as it contorted into forced laughter to try and mask his fury. "Shall we dance?" she said to end this treacherous conversation.

With that, and feeling trapped for the moment, he agreed and they joined in the waltz. He would rather have struck her for her blackmail than dance with her but had little choice. He despised her but conceded she knew too much. He decided then that he would silently leave the manor once the hide and seek started, this would give him cover and by the time anyone noticed he would be long gone. He also considered the note he had received from Lovell, asking him to meet him in the summerhouse by the lake. He would perhaps go and do this quickly, to have a parting word with his friend and lover. Even though they had made an agreement to never meet or communicate again once this day was over, he would use the opportunity to reinforce the pact and also to warn him about Charlotte. Her mind, he feared, was unbalanced and would wreak havoc yet on his marriage to Ellen should the opportunity present itself.

Meanwhile, I was glad to see Father so happy and dancing so well! He whispered something in my ear to see what I thought of the idea and I laughed delightedly at the prospect of his desire. I then watched, with Lovell at my side, as he strode across to Florence, who was standing by the main entrance to the ballroom, happily watching discreetly as the dances progressed.

"My dear, Florence," said Father to her, "you have been my daughters' worthy governess, guardian and friend for all these years. Nobody could have ever replaced their mother, but you have come as close as anyone could. For that I will be eternally grateful to you."

"Sir!" said a startled and not a little embarrassed Florence, "please keep your voice down in case any one hears you." She looked at him smiling brightly at her and was puzzled. She felt her cheeks colouring. "I did only my duty and the pleasure in helping you and your daughters was all mine, I assure you."

"Florence, enough of this formal chatter. Would you do me the honour of dancing a waltz with me to celebrate my daughter's wedding? Apart from her and Charlotte, there is no other I wish to dance with on this special day." He held his arm out to her in preparation of escorting her to the floor.

"Baron! Have you lost control of yourself? I am a mere house-keeper and have no place dancing with you in public. What would people think – and say?"

"Be dammed with what they may or may not think. I want to dance a waltz with you and dance a waltz I will!"

His protestation left her no choice but to meekly oblige and take his arm. They crossed into the centre of the floor and whilst everyone watched, they began a waltz that delighted us all to see. If anyone deserved such an honour at my wedding, it was darling Florence. Without her, I imagine we would have not flourished as we had – and neither would Willow Manor. In spite of her reluctance, Florence's eyes were filled with tears at this remarkable gesture accorded her by Father. It said much, dear reader and friend about their closeness and their private relationship that would never be revealed to the world. I only tell you now because the story of that past requires it of me.

Once the dancing had exhausted everyone and Andrews had served refreshments, together with the other house staff, of mulled wine, champagne and such like, it was at last time to think about the game of hide and seek. Sometimes I felt it was only me that relished this part of the wedding day, but I have to include Charlotte, as she seemed as enthusiastic as I was about the prospect. Obviously her motives were not as mine – little did I know!

Father gathered everyone together, including, at my insistence, the house servants and asked for their attention. With great humour and delight he explained that it was traditional for the bride to run off and hide and then Lovell, helped by other guests, would chase after me to seek my whereabouts! The exceptions to this physical game would be himself and Lady Marlborough, and anyone else of a certain age, not used to such dashing around and running up and down stairs – their respective ages barring them from such exertion.

He then asked them all to turn away and cover their eyes with their hands. Lovell would, he then instructed, count to 100. As soon as he started this count, I would run off and seek my secret hiding place – my hope, dear reader and friend was that Lovell would of course be the first to find me! Charlotte had aided me in this desire by a conversation we had had earlier about this and how I could achieve that wish.

"Charlotte, I want Lovell to be able to find me first, but can't think how I can do this without spoiling the game for him. What should I do?" I had asked.

"Oh, Ellen you can be such a foolish ninny at times," she said with a laugh. "There is always a way to do everything if you try hard enough and think it through."

"Well?" I asked expectantly. "What should I do to contrive this?"

"Well, I suppose the best thing is for you to make your way to my rooms and wait in my dressing room. No one will think of searching there first and you don't want anyone to find you too quickly, as we need to build the suspense for Lovell and everyone else don't we?"

"Indeed we do," I agreed, "but why your rooms? Once there I will be trapped and unable to move anywhere else in the manor without being seen."

"That, dear sister is where you are wrong. From my dressing room there is a little used servants' staircase that leads to the attic – it is concealed behind the oak panelling of my dressing room and hardly anyone knows about it."

"Perfect," I said as I clapped my hands in delight at this information. "It will help me to hide well but how will Lovell find me – he would never know of such a secret staircase?"

"Don't worry about that, I will make sure he finds his way to the attic through another servants' staircase, from the main bedroom corridor in that wing. I will lead him to you, dear sister."

She smiled conspiratorially and then hugged me close, as if to reassure me that all would be well and our plan would have the desired effect and reunite me with my husband, Lovell at a given time. Thus it was planned – I had a hand in my own fate!

Oh the mistletoe bough!
Oh the mistletoe bride!

Lovell and Nicholai found themselves standing in the cavernous dereliction that had once been the ballroom of Willow Manor. Having entered through the main front doors, or what remained of them, they moved through the hall and passed the grand staircase to make their way to this part of the house – as elsewhere, all opulence or grandeur was driven to dust. Some small fragments of the once huge mirrors remained, heavily foxed and dulled by decades of the unfettered elements gaining easy entrance and doing their worst.

As they stood looking around in some awe, because the house still had the ability to create wonder in the mind of the beholder – in spite of its sorry state, I noticed that their reflections were those of their Victorian incarnations. Lovell was just as handsome as he had always been and his presence here lifted me. Although, it was something of an anti-climax as there had been no rush of longed for relief, or sudden freedom, or happiness now he was here again.

"What was that," whispered Nicholai to Lovell, "did you hear it too?"

"Yes, it sounded like voices chanting some kind of verse."

"Perhaps that is where the fire is lit – and explains the smoking chimney?"

"She is here isn't she – the mistletoe bride? Can you sense her too, Nicholai?"

"How did you know about her?"

"It's long been a legend in my family about what happened here and how it sent my great-great-uncle mad. The tragedy was never fully explained, I understand."

"You have a connection to this place as well? So does Charley, so it seems that you two have something in common."

"The ghost of Lady Ellen Forsyth is supposed to haunt this place and roam the manor for eternity waiting the return of her Lord Lovell. The tragedy involved a Russian Count as well – maybe that's where you fit in?"

"Don't say that." Nicholai shuddered and then considered me. "Maybe this is her lucky day then? How come you never mentioned this before?"

"It never occurred to me – why are you so interested anyway?

"I came here with Charley, that day I told you about and it was very weird – I could swear then, and I could swear again now, that we are being watched. Something is here, I can feel it for sure."

"I heard about the place but I have never been before – why would I? It needs demolishing before it falls down. We can be too sentimental about these old places in England."

"Work is starting in the new year to restore it and turn it into luxury apartments."

I was shocked to hear them discuss my home with such indifference. Then Nicholai's telephone began to ring. He answered it and I could hear Charlotte's voice coming from it.

"Where are you, Nicholai?" she asked abruptly, "I don't want a wasted journey on Christmas Eve afternoon."

"We're at the manor already – we're waiting for you."

"Oh, I take it Lovell is also there then? I thought you wanted to speak with me."

"I do! We do, I should say. We just want to sort things out and hopefully move forward so we can be friends."

"The traffic is really crap, I am just on the Banbury road heading out of Oxford – so should be about twenty minutes or so if the traffic allows."

"That's great, we'll see you soon. Drive carefully."

He clicked off his telephone and put it in his pocket. In her car, Charley headed towards us at Willow Manor, her reflection in the rear view mirror was that of Charlotte from 1893. Soon we would all be together again.

Oh the mistletoe bough!
Oh the mistletoe bride!

As my guests and family began to count I ran off through the house and made a play of going hither and thither in case anyone was listening. I ran up the great staircase and across the minstrel gallery, towards the wing of the house that provided accommodations for Charlotte and myself. Once in Charlotte's room, I quickly slipped into her dressing room and closed the door behind myself. All I had to do then was wait for Charlotte to arrive.

Soon I could hear the clatter of feet and the shrieks of laughter, as everyone began to disperse throughout the manor in an attempt to find me. The sounds were both near and far, so in those moments I feared being discovered too quickly and by the wrong person.

Nicholai had used this diversion to give his instructions to Andrews to ready his coach and four. His luggage had been packed and loaded as planned. Nicholai made his way outside and crossed the lawns leading to the summerhouse by the lake. He could see the shadow of Rodgers, who he thought was Lovell, waiting for him there, not realizing it was another trap initiated by Charlotte. Suddenly he stopped and thought better of this meeting. He had to get away and as painful as it was he could not face his loss again. Better to leave Lovell to his new life and leave this place for good. That is what he did. He returned and boarded his coach and instructed the driver to depart with haste. Little did he know it, but he managed to escape death that night. As his carriage dashed off down the drive, Andrews rushed from the house and watched, slightly bemused that no greeting of farewell had been given and no words of thanks or apology were to be relayed to the Baron from Count Nicholai, due to his unorthodox departure.

In Charlotte's dressing room I was startled to see a section of the oak panelling begin to creak and move, it shook me and as I was about to scream in fear the secret door opened and Charlotte stood before me with a grin of satisfaction on her face. In the moment I forgot she would enter this way. In the distance we could make out people calling my name – I was sure I heard Lovell close by and implored my sister to help me hide, to make sure he didn't find me too quickly.

"Come this way, follow me," said Charlotte who turned and went from whence she appeared seconds before. The candle she held flickered erratically and cast an odd, looming shadow across the dark, secret staircase that led up into the service corridors and attic rooms. I huddled my dress in one arm and began to follow her. "Mind you don't trip and make any noise or you'll give us away," she whispered.

"My dress will be ruined," I heard myself mutter. "Why did we have to come this way?"

"You wanted it to be a good hiding place and I needed to make sure you could get here without being seen, silly girl!"

"I'm sorry, I hate this dark staircase, that's all," I replied meekly, "I never knew you had that secret panel in your room. How long have you known about that?"

"I make it my business to know everything about this house," she said rather haughtily. "I like to know exactly what is going on and who goes where!"

This was typical of Charlotte and her obsession with details. I could not have cared less if I was never privy to secret staircases and doors and the movements of the servants within the manor. Perhaps, I found myself thinking, this was why she was so good at running the house and estate for Father.

After several twists and turns of the cramped staircase, we eventually emerged in a bare corridor. Immediately the candle-light helped to open out the space, making it feel less cramped and claustrophobic. Charlotte led the way down the corridor.

"Careful not to make much noise, the bare floor boards make every footstep a possible giveaway."

As she said it my foot fell on a loose board that creaked loudly and brought us both to a sudden halt. It seemed we instinctively held our breaths and listened to see if it had given us away. In that moment I wondered at the extent of the Manor – I had never been to these dark, windowless corridors before. I found myself giggling out loud and instantly tried to suppress it, as I knew it would annoy Charlotte, especially after the trouble she had taken to help me.

"How far are we from the main house, Charlotte," I asked suddenly fearful that her proposed hiding place would be too remote. "It seems far off, going on the muffled sound of distant voices still searching for me," I said in a whisper.

"Don't worry, it is adjacent to the main bedroom corridor of our wing, not far from your sitting room actually," she added. This last piece of information immediately gave me some comfort of sorts.

"Here we are," she said as she reached a door and opened it, "in here, be quick as we haven't much time."

The room also had bare floors and to the right there was a short flight of stairs, leading down to what I assumed was the main corridor of this wing. The door at the top of these stairs Charlotte closed immediately. Placing her candle on an old table, she presented me with the huge, linen chest standing in one corner of the room. The lid was open.

"Here we are," she said with delight, "didn't I tell you I would find somewhere perfect for you to hide?"

I crossed and looked into the chest and admired the pink silk lining and it looked quite spacious. I hesitated because I feared it would be too obscure a place and that Lovell would never find me here. Charlotte must have read my mind.

"Don't worry," she said reassuringly, "I have thought of everything, dear Ellen. Once you are hidden in the chest, I shall go and join the others and if it seems Lovell will not venture here, I will lead him without him knowing of my contrivance."

With that, dear reader and friend I was reassured. Charlotte helped me as I first stood in the open chest and then just as I was about to say something in protest of being closed in, the handle of the door at the bottom of the service stairs began to rattle and the door bang. It showed the determination of the person intent on opening it.

From that point everything happened so quickly. I sat down and then Charlotte helped smooth my dress within the chest as I clasped my mistletoe corsage tightly. She helped to make me comfortable. The door below seemed to be pushed open and she very abruptly shut the lid. (This left a small piece of my dress and a sprig of mistletoe trapped in the join). Once she had done so, she sat on the chest and carefully closed the spring locks shut. This meant of course that I was trapped and unable to open the lid from within. With that task completed she covered the chest with an old dust sheet, picked up the candle, opened the door, and made her way down the stairs to meet none other than dearest Lovell.

"Any sign of her?" he asked looking past her up the stairs. "I have searched high and low and I cannot find her."

"No," replied Charlotte, "she is not this way. We must look in a less obvious place perhaps?" This was her chilling reply, knowing she had left me to my fate, locked in that linen chest.

Oh, the mistletoe bough!
Oh, the mistletoe bride!

They sought her that night,
They sought her next day,
They sought her in vain when a week passed away,
In the highest, the lowest, the loneliest spot,
Young Lovell sought wildly,
But found her not!

The chanting guided Lovell and Nicholai to the room at the far end of the corridor, leading from the minstrel's gallery at the top of the grand staircase. They moved with caution and pushed aside the occasional cobweb and clump of rubbish and leaves, trying hard not to be heard by those inside the room.

Florence was still in some kind of trance and Millie and Rodgers were responding to her instructions. Florence's face became fluid as wax once again and contorted and twisted as she began to moan, quietly at first, but becoming more distressed as the spirit that had decided to channel her became more impatient to be heard. Her voice deepened and began to growl and reverberate.

Lovell and Nicholai had reached the door and were listening intently to what was going on inside. Suddenly the door was snatched from Lovell's hand and flew open, leaving them exposed and seen by those inside. I watched carefully as I passed them and could see Florence's face transform into that of my father. Her voice deepened with masculinity as she groaned and then Father looked around the room before he spoke.

"Where is the Russian?" he demanded in angry tones I had hardly heard him use in life. "Why did he take my daughter – why did he take you, Ellen? I know you are here, Ellen. You must listen to me and go to the lake. Go to the lake. I will deal with the Russian."

At this point Nicholai walked into the room and Father's features contorted and his anger was almost apoplectic.

"I hope you burn in hell for what you did, sir! My daughter had done you no harm. She was an innocent, an innocent, and you took her from me and her husband."

Nicholai had walked forward and, by his reflection in the mirror fragment, he was Nicholai of 1893.

"I did nothing to your daughter, sir. Why would I? She was my friend's bride. What do you accuse me of sir?"

"Don't lie to me – you took her and spirited her away. We never saw her or you again. If it was not you, tell me how that could be, Nicholai, tell me…"

"I did nothing to your daughter, Baron. I left only because I wanted to leave and return to Russia. This I agreed with Lovell, our disagreement was private and didn't involve anyone else."

It was at this moment I appeared to them. I crossed the window and moved towards the far side of the room, by the fireplace, where they could all see me. Their reactions were at first ones of horror, as they saw me as a near skeletal corpse walking before them.

"Father," I said, "Nicholai did me no harm. I never left this place, I never left Willow Manor. It is not he you should be angry with."

"Child, you are lost and abandoned in this place. We still search for you here and cannot rest until we find you. Your mother and I are so sad and lost without you."

"Lady Ellen," said Millie suddenly, "we are all connected with you, that is why we are here, to try and set you free. To help you…"

"I am no longer there," I said, "I am no longer in the place of my death. The chest is still in the attic. My remains are not there – only my spirit roams this place."

Lovell stepped forward and into the room. He gazed at me with eyes that suggested what he saw was the beauty I had on our wedding day, so long ago. The warmth and affection stunned me and there were tears slowly falling down his cheeks.

"What fff-fate befell you, Ellen? What horror did you experience? What evil did this to you and cursed you here for all this time?" He turned and looked at the Baron, sobbing. "Nicholai did no harm ttt-to Ellen, sir. It is perhaps closer to your own hearth you need to look. He left that night because we had made an agreement never to see or communicate with each other again. If anyone betrayed Ellen, it was I."

Lovell collapsed in sobs and Nicholai quickly supported him to a window ledge, so he could sit, and then placed a protective arm around his shoulders.

"It is Charlotte, I fear, that had her hand in this, sir. Did you ask her what had become of Ellen? If so what did she say?"

"Charlotte was as devastated as I was at the loss of her sister. She knew nothing, only that she had seen you and Ellen conspiring to run away together to Russia."

"That was a lie, sir!" Nicholai turned and looked directly at me. "You must tell him, Ellen. Why are you protecting Charlotte after what she did?"

"It is true, Father," I said at last with all eyes upon me. "Charlotte guided me during hide and seek to find a place. I thought she was helping me have a game with Lovell. She closed the lid of the linen chest in the attic and never opened it again. I soon became silent through lack of air, my desperation to escape was in vain and my scratching at the lid heard by no one. My sister murdered me and felt no remorse or pity for what she had done to me."

Florence groaned and suddenly shrieked in her familiar voice and then her head collapsed onto the table. Everyone was quiet and just stared at her, not quite knowing what would happen next.

"I was to murder you, sir," Rodgers said to Nicholai. "Charlotte arranged for you to meet Lord Lovell at the summerhouse, but she had forged the letter. It was me who waited but you never came. I had orders to slit your throat and to dump you in the lake."

"I don't understand," said Millie, "why would Miss Charlotte do those terrible things? I know she hated some of the servants, but this?"

"She knew exactly what she was doing, Ellen," said Nicholai. "She had tried her best to seduce me, then Lovell, behind your back, and when she couldn't get what she wanted, conspired to murder us and have Lovell for herself."

"He speaks the truth, Ellen," said Florence sitting up and looking at me. Her voice was the familiar voice of my own dear Florence of long ago. "I blame myself, I knew she was mixed up in her mind, jealous and vengeful, but did nothing as I thought I could protect her and control her and once you and Lord Lovell married she would settle down."

"I don't understand why I am no longer there. What happened to me as my remains are no longer in the chest? The chest that was my tomb remains in the attic." I looked at them all and felt overcome with the horror of my own fate, probably for the first time. "Did you marry her, Lovell? I can't remember much after my own death and very little until I saw you commit suicide in the summerhouse…"

"Yes, I ddd-did marry Charlotte eventually, bbb-but only through necessity. We lived in this house but it was mostly closed up as we had less and less money. Your father and Lady Marlborough were ddd-dead within the year of your disappearance. Your father of a broken heart – your loss was too much for him. Charlotte bore a child, but it was Rodgers, the stable groom, who sired it. Thankfully we concealed it from your father and he never knew of the child's illegitimacy. We bbb-brought her up as best we could, so married for the sake of propriety. There was no love, no intimacy, no warmth, as that was only yours."

"Where is Charlotte," asked Millie. "The rest of us are here but where is she?"

"She is not far away," said Florence, her face once again fluid like wax and contorting into odd shapes. "She is returning to the scene of her crimes at last."

Millie suddenly began to chant again the next verse from the song. Trancelike her staring eyes fixed on me as if I would disappear from her view.

Oh, the mistletoe bough!
Oh, the mistletoe bride!

The years passed by and their grief at last
Was told as a sorrowful tale long past
When Lovell appeared, all the children cried,
'See the old man weeps for his bride!'

Oh, the mistletoe bride!
Oh, the mistletoe bride!

At length an old chest that had long lain hid
Was found in the attic, they raised the lid.
A skeletal form lay mouldering there,
In the bridal wreath of the lady fair!

That last part was wrong. They never found my remains. I watched as Florence became more agitated and began to groan and howl, as if a phantom in fury had seized her soul and was suffocating its evil. Her features took on the appearance of her ancestor again and she smiled kindly at me, then Father, Mother and even my darling aunt's face appeared one after the other until Florence's features returned and smiled again at me.

"You must go to the lake, Ellen. Do you understand me?" she said as if it was an instruction that could not be disobeyed.

"Why? Why does everyone ask me to go to the lake? I was always told not to go near the lake because it was dangerous when you are alone," I said with fear in my voice. "I hate the mists and the water unnerves me..."

"I dd-don't understand either," said Lovell, "why must she gg-go to the lake?"

"Quiet!" demanded Florence, "look into your mind's eye, all of you. Concentrate, she has arrived. She is back!"

We all closed our eyes as she instructed. After a few moments we could hear the sound of a car engine roaring in the distance. Charlotte was approaching in her horseless carriage on the main Oxford Road, beyond the sign newly erected.

"Concentrate and you will see her," said Florence. "You must all witness this, it is the only way we can set Ellen free of this place and allow her to move to eternity in peace. Focus on Charlotte, focus on your relationship with her and connect to her to help me. The more energy I can draw on the easier this will be to resolve and set Ellen free at last."

Dear reader and friend, I cannot speak for the others, but this is what I saw. I could see out of the rear-view mirror in Charlotte's carriage as she approached the manor gates at speed. Her face was set like granite so she was angry or displeased at her current circumstances. As I looked out I could feel the force coming from Florence back in the Manor and Charlotte became aware that the locks on her doors suddenly snapped closed. She frantically pushed buttons and tried handles but to no avail, they were locked tight. It was then she realized the speed of her carriage was increasing beyond her control. She watched, helpless, as the speed indicator rose alarmingly and there was nothing she could do to stop it. Her feet pounded the pedals in vain.

I opened my eyes and was back in the room with Florence and the others, they were all moaning, the sweat evident on their brows. Only Florence had her eyes open and she stared hard out through the window; her face shuddering under the strain.

Closing my eyes again I was back in the carriage and watching Charlotte as she tried to open the windows but nothing happened at her command, like the doors they were locked shut. I could begin to see her fear. She tried to twist the wheel of the carriage but it did not respond and drove on seemingly of its own accord, at greater speed than ever. As it passed the gatehouse it veered out of control and then hit a grass bank, heavily frozen due to the time of year, that acted as a catapult and it launched the carriage through a boundary wall that crumbled instantly and allowed the speeding carriage to continue unabated through the grounds of Willow Manor. It headed towards the lake, the carriage roaring as it accelerated to again increase the speed.

I opened my eyes and found myself standing watching by the window. All but Florence now seemed exhausted and collapsed onto the floor and across the table. Florence remained alone, her frame shuddering and jolting as she concentrated all her energies on the task at hand. I turned and watched as the carriage with Charlotte trapped inside hurtled towards the old summerhouse. The outcome was inevitable.

The carriage smashed into and demolished the summerhouse then dove into the lake. It slowly sank. I closed my eyes and watched again through her rear-view mirror within the carriage. She scratched and fought at the doors and windows but could not free herself. The car sank down and down into the depth of the lake. The windows began to crack and water poured in. Charlotte screamed in vain. No one could hear her. She slowly found the water covering her face and knowing she was drowning. She could see weak beams of sunshine above, piercing the water.

As the car hit the bottom of the lake, she could no longer hold her breath, but knew that the moment she opened her mouth her lungs would fill with freezing water. Her fingers clawed weakly at the door handle, her strength now gone.

The car had disturbed a trunk buried in the silt on the lake bottom. The lid disintegrated and the silt swirled around as she watched in those last moments. From within came my wedding dress and veil, wrapped still in my skeletal remains. The swirling water created by her carriage gave them an eerie life, as they floated past her open eyes, as if I occupied them once again with living flesh. A macabre dance ensued as I ascended elegantly to the surface and was illuminated by the last rays of sunlight to break through the cloud on that cold Christmas Eve. As I rose, the whole story flashed before me – similar to how, as the saying goes, one's life would whilst drowning.

As I broke the surface of the murky waters of the lake with a gasp of release, I realized I was at last free. I could finally move on and leave behind this world I no longer cared for, nor ever wanted to be part of. I had just one more task to complete, my friend, and that was to relay to you this story – so make of it what you will.

The mystery was solved. Charlotte had moved my remains to another chest and had it dumped in the lake. This protected her further from discovery and also enabled her to perpetuate the myth that I had run away, or been forced to leave with Nicholai. She did it in the same cold blooded way she gladly murdered me, by suffocation and entrapment.

As for Lovell and Nicholai? The love they had for each other in 1893 was impossible for them to explore, or live openly with. Indeed I did not know then that such things existed between two men. I was ignorant of many things. Lovell, I know, did love me and would have been a faithful husband and friend, but he would only have ever been in love with one person – Nicholai. Charlotte entrapped him but in a different way. His marriage to her was out of kindness to the child that was Charley's grand-mother. The line ends now as she thankfully had no children of her own.

I loved them both, Lovell and Nicholai, and still do, but in a different way. Perhaps in this life, they will be able to enjoy that love in a way that will embrace all those lost emotions of their past. That is my hope for them.

They will remember little of this when they wake in the room of that derelict manor that was once my home. The only person who will understand the full story is you my friend. For that I thank you. I will never forget you and hope that each Christmas Eve you will think of me fondly and remember me in the time and place in which I belong – a young woman from 1893, full of excitement at the prospect of being a Mistletoe Bride and married on Christmas Eve.

Epilogue: Yet to Come!

Willow Manor was transformed into a luxury development of residential and retirement apartments, along with a lakeside restaurant. The interior of the manor became unrecognizable, apart from the grand entrance hall and staircase and the adjoining drawing room that was allocated as public space for those who owned apartments. In these areas their respective guests could wait for them, and residents could meet for coffee mornings or other events. It reflected the history of the manor, and its previous grandeur, and would at least be a home of sorts again as opposed to the crumbling dereliction that had nearly destroyed it.

In the drawing room with its large Georgian windows looking out over the gardens and the distant lake, the ambiance was once again of refined comfort and elegance. Above the fireplace my fresco portrait remained intact and after restoration was as vibrant as the day my father unveiled it on Christmas Eve 1893. It was a permanent reminder of the legend surrounding my fate.

The grounds of the manor offer an inviting choice of walks into the meadows and woods beyond – all once again manicured and maintained to the highest standards. The old summerhouse has been replaced with a large and pleasant restaurant overlooking the lake, that is open to residents and visitors alike. Even a part of the stables has been restored to offer horse riding and other leisure activities.

Beyond is the village of Minster Lovell. Its cottages and church have changed little in more than a century, they overlook the ruins of the medieval manor that has become a place for young lovers to court and sometimes carve their initials into the stones to declare everlasting love. I like that very much.

Florence came to live in a retirement apartment in the complex when she gave up working at the Randolph Hotel. She had always had an affinity with her ancestor of the same name and found she felt comfortable living in the manor – it was oddly reassuring and familiar to her. Millie and Rodgers married and accepted a job as caretakers for the retirement section of the manor and the many elderly residents. They too enjoyed the link with history because their ancestors had also worked for the estate.

The story goes that if the light is right, and especially in the days leading up to Christmas, from the corner of your eye, you may fleetingly observe a severe looking young woman dressed in Victorian clothes. She can be seen in the drawing room gazing up at my portrait, or standing by the lakeside looking out as if searching for something. That will be Charlotte. Take no notice of her. She will do you no harm.

About The Author & Playwright

David was born in Oxford, England, in 1959. He graduated from London's **City University** with a **BA (Hons) Degree** in Journalism. In addition to this he has a Teaching Degree from **Lancaster University** and a **Masters Degree** in the Arts from the **University of Central Lancashire**. He continues his professional development with courses at the **University of Oxford.** Prior to this he attended **London Theatre Arts** to study drama, and then worked extensively in the performing arts industry as a playwright, producer and director. His stage plays include the award winning **Forever Nineteen, After The Tone** and **The Post Card** – which enjoyed London and New York productions, as well as touring nationally in the United Kingdom. His involvement in adapting the libretto for Ivor Novello's 1935 musical **Glamorous Night** resulted in him directing the 50th Anniversary Concert to celebrate the life and work of Novello at the Theatre Royal, Drury Lane, in London's West End. Subsequently he has worked as the **Ivor Novello** Consultant on **Julian Fellowes** and **Robert Altman's Oscar** and **BAFTA** winning film **Gosford Park**, and contributed to the BBC Documentary on the life of Novello, **The Handsomest Man in Britain.** He is the author of **In Search of Ruritania**, a biography on Ivor Novello – featured on **BBC Radio 2** as part of the **Great War Centenary** celebrations 2014. **Anything But Merry! The Life and Times of Lily Elsie** the Edwardian actress and singer who found fame in Lehar's **The Merry Widow**; the novel **The Mistletoe Haunting – legend of Minster Lovell**, and **Mildred on the Marne: Mildred Aldrich, Front-line Witness 1914-1918.** Currently completed a new play based on the relationship between opera composer Puccini and his wife titled **Elvira & I – Puccini's Scandalous Passions!** And working on a new biography based on the life of Martita Hunt (*Miss Haversham in*

David Lean's 1947 film of Great Expectations) titled: **Greater Than Expectations: The Life and Times of Martita Hunt.**

Further information available at: www.christyplays.com

Also by David Slattery-Christy

Non Fiction
Mildred on the Marne: Mildred Aldrich Front-line
Witness 1914-1918
In Search of Ruritania: The Life & Times of Ivor Novello
Anything But Merry! The Life & Times of Lily Elsie
Edwardian Beauty: Lily Elsie & The Merry Widow

Plays
Elvira & I – Puccini's Scandalous Passions!
Glamorous Night
Forever Nineteen
The Post Card
After The Tone

www.christyplays.com

COSMIC
EGG
BOOKS

If you prefer to spend your nights with Vampires and Werewolves rather than the mundane then we publish the books for you. If your preference is for Dragons and Faeries or Angels and Demons – we should be your first stop. Perhaps your perfect partner has artificial skin or comes from another planet – step right this way. Our curiosity shop contains treasures you will enjoy unearthing. If your passion is Fantasy (including magical realism and spiritual fantasy), Horror or Science Fiction (including Steampunk), Cosmic Egg books will feed your hunger.